Poison,

Perennials,

and a Poltergeist

Also by Tina D.C. Hayes

No More Tears

ROCK CANDY ROMANTIC SUSPENSE
Nefarious

PETAL PUSHERS MYSTERY SERIES
Secrets, Snapdragons, and a Spirit

Poison,

Perennials,

and a Poltergeist

Petal Pushers Mystery Series, Book 1

Tina D. C. Hayes

Hazy Moon Ink

This is a work of fiction. Names, characters, places, and incidents are a product of the author's imagination or are used fictitiously. Any resemblance to actual events, locales, or persons, living or dead, is completely coincidental.

Copyright © 2013 by Tina D. C. Hayes.

ISBN-13: 978-0692362181
ISBN-10: 0692362185

2nd Edition

Hazy Moon Ink

To my parents and grandparents, for raising me to love books and follow my dreams;

To my children, for showing me the little magic moments tucked into each day;

To my husband, for encouraging me even when he wished I'd hush up about plot lines, revisions, and Miss Addie;

And to Maizy, my Boston terrier BFF, now an angel, for sitting with me all those countless hours as I wrote.

Prologue

My beautiful home, reduced to a cobweb-infested wreck. All the flowers gone, every last bush and potted plant, dead and withered Lord only knows how long ago. The neighbors must think I've done lost my mind.

How long has it been? Just wait til I get my hands on whoever's responsible for this ungodly mess. Looks like nary a soul's been here in forever, let alone thought to pick up a mop or dust rag. Cain't remember who was left in charge, but mercy sakes alive, somebody's gonna catch it over this. Don't know what in the world they were thinking, lettin' things go this way. Where the dickens is my furniture?

This house never felt so lonely before. Neither have I, truth be told. Seems almost like I cain't tell the difference between hours and days anymore, like time's just a racin' past me. I need the sun to shine down on me again, to warm the chill out of these ole bones and set things right. Plenty of folks 'round here I still need to see to or straighten out.

Instead, I'm all cooped up like a brood hen with nary an egg under her feathered fanny. Got to get my bearings, run my fingers over the one thing that can help me.

It's gone! Bad enough my world turned upside down, but this is the last straw. I swany, my heart just broke in two and fell to the pit of my stomach. When did it disappear, and who could've took it? I have to get it back.

A change is on the way, something in my bones is tellin' me so. One thing I do know. Come hell or high water, I will take back what's mine. Lord have mercy on anybody who stands in my way.

Chapter One

January

*There came a time when the risk
to remain tight in the bud was more painful
than the risk it took to blossom.*
~ Anais Nin

"Petal Pushers, Darci Shelton speaking. How may I help you?" Enthusiastic to see whether her first order would be for a flower arrangement or a live plant, she'd answered the phone on the first ring. Her voice was a bit less cheerful a few seconds later. "Sorry, you must have the wrong number. Nobody named Guido lives here."

Darci put the 'Open' sign in the front window, adjusting it to hang perfectly straight between the lacy white curtains. Then she decided it might look better slightly askew and angled it to the side. She felt a silly grin spread across her face as she circuited the shop to make sure the floral displays and potted plants projected the best possible first impression for her new customers, if any actually showed up today.

She arranged donuts and plastic coffee cups on the counter and hoped they wouldn't go to waste. Gimmicks to pull people into the store were actually kind of fun, and she had plenty of them planned for this first crucial year. A newspaper ad and flyers placed around town advertised free coffee, donuts, and a package of seeds for everyone who came to the grand opening. A wicker basket beside the coffee carafe held the freebees. Her business card, tied to each seed packet with a jute twine bow, would remind customers to visit the shop again around planting time.

A bell jingling on the door announced the arrival of Petal Pushers' first customer. A man in his mid-twenties walked around the display tables, looking confused.

"What can I help you with today?" Darci tried not to sound as giddy as she felt. She busied her hands with a loose piece of eucalyptus to keep her fidgeting under control.

"Um, well," he said, rubbing the back of his head, "I was thinking about taking my wife some flowers."

"You came to the right place, then. Did you have something specific in mind?"

"Yep." A sheepish grin turned up the corner of his mouth. "Something that'll make her forget she's mad at me."

4

"I won't even ask what you did." Darci hoped to put the guy at ease with her smile. "Just tell me how much you want to spend and I'll whip up a nice bouquet for you."

"Twenty-five bucks?"

"No problem. Help yourself to some donuts." She guided him toward the refreshments that took up half the front counter, then headed for the workroom and the bins of fresh cut flowers. "I'll be right back."

Darci returned with a bouquet of pink rose-buds and dainty purple blossoms. She hoped she hadn't gone overboard with all the baby's breath and greenery. "That'll be twenty-two fifty." When he reached for his wallet, she added, "Go ahead and have another donut and some coffee for the road, since you're my very first customer."

"Thanks, but this hangover is putting a damper on my appetite." His pale complexion and blood-shot eyes confirmed his statement.

"Sorry. Can I get you an aspirin or anything?" With any luck, maybe he'd go partying and piss the little lady off every weekend this year. Darci would gladly jump through fire hoops for some regular customers. Handing him his change, she felt guilty for her thoughts. Sort of. She walked him to the door and presented him with his free package of nasturtium seeds. "Have a nice day, and please come again."

Her husband Wade warned her that New Year's Day might not be the most ideal time to hold a grand opening. She hadn't cared then and she didn't care now. It was all part of the business plan she'd drawn up months earlier. Petal Pushers flower shop had exactly one calendar year to become a successful business or she'd sell it, cut her losses, and go back to some god-awful nine-to-five job she hated. The very thought of that made her stomach ache.

When she'd worked as a sales clerk at a department store, she kept a journal under the counter. Every free minute went to sketching out plans for her dream of opening this flower shop. She worked out all the details on paper long ago- her business plan, sales gimmicks, a 'Plant of the Month' page for her company website, what to keep in stock during which season, even how many employees she thought she'd need. She'd lugged around a stack of gardening books so she could study different types of plants, learn tricks for improving her natural green thumb, and get a better feel for creating wreaths and floral arrangements.

It took her a while to save the startup money. Besides a sales job she loathed, she'd scraped and saved every chance she had. Weekends babysitting a total brat from down the street added to her savings account, though she had to deduct money to stock up on Excedrin for the little fart's visits. She recycled every empty aluminum can she got her hands on and became a bargain hunter extraordinaire. Her family never found name brands on anything in their cabinets, just generic stuff like Fruity-O cereal and Savvy shampoo. Five years of scrimping, saving, and clipping coupons helped fill her nest egg with enough money to put her plan into action.

She could have taken the easy way out when her husband offered to help finance the shop, but Darci resolved to do it by herself. She wanted to make deposits into their joint bank account and her son's college fund. Darci had never lived on her own and needed the security of knowing she could support herself if anything happened to Wade.

Darci bit her lip, remembering when her mother became a widow with a teenage daughter to support. The financial struggle turned her beautiful mom into a gray-haired waitress on food stamps. Mary Dubois never complained. She'd pretended to enjoy her job at the restaurant, but Darci heard her crying at night when extra expenses came up, like school fees or outgrown shoes. Darci had a happy childhood, but often wondered how things would have been if her father hadn't drowned when she was thirteen.

She lifted a silver picture frame from a display table, then peered at the image before hugging it to her chest. "I sure am missing you today, Daddy." After John Dubois died, Darci spent more time than usual outside. She could almost feel his touch through his old gardening gloves as she pulled weeds and staked tomato plants. Her work in the vegetable garden he loved so much made her feel closer to him, almost as if he might come bounding out of the shed pushing a wheelbarrow any minute.

Her love of growing things, along with her fear of financial disaster, spawned the idea of opening her own flower shop, a notion never far from her thoughts. Looking around the shop this morning, Darci could still hardly believe what luck she'd had finding this place. Vacant for decades before the owners decided to put it on the market, the house was in pretty decent structural shape to be over a hundred years old. It was small, but with more than enough room. The upstairs, with its cute dormers and low ceilings, was the perfect place for her son to do his homework or play video games without bothering or getting bothered by her customers. She could cook herself a hot lunch every day in the huge kitchen on the main floor, which would also serve as extra workspace. The cellar, with its old-fashioned outside entrance, provided a lot of storage space, even if it was kind of creepy down there.

A few older ladies drifted in through the morning. Darci figured the free food lured them there, as well as their curiosity about the renovations to the old building.

Sleeping with a carpenter helped keep the overhead down. Wade cleared his schedule for the past two weeks to help get everything ready for opening day. He repaired the roof, installed a counter, and set up the computer while she potted plants and whipped up displays. Paxton, her nine-year-old son, was a bit overenthusiastic helping her paint the walls, splattering Darci's dark brown hair with buttery yellow highlights. The heavy-duty drop cloths she'd sprung for turned out to be a good investment, since they saved her from having to refinish the wooden floors.

It took forever to find the perfect shade of yellow, but the warm color on the walls made her feel cozy each time she saw it. Darci never knew there were so many different hues until she brought home a collection of paint samples. A dizzying myriad of cheery shades bridged the gap between 'hint of yellow' and 'Egyptian gold', some so barely discernable from the surrounding squares that she had to squint, holding the card out at arm's length to find any differences.

After narrowing down the paint selection to the final three colors, she'd taped the swatches side by side on the wall in the workroom and asked everyone to look them over and give their opinion. So similar were 'daffodil', 'summer sunshine', and 'Indian sunflower', nobody could choose a favorite . . . or gave a crap, she thought now, smiling at the memory. When 'daffodil' was ahead by two votes, Paxton begged everyone who walked through the door to pick the color on the left so he could quit hearing about the dang swatches. That worked, but Darci decided to go with the one on the far right instead. She liked the name 'Indian sunflower' better because sunflowers had a longer blooming season than the shorter-lived Easter flowers. Made perfect sense to her.

Her inability to make decisions made Wade and Paxton groan at the mention of a shopping trip. For example, back-to-school time this past fall had them standing in a crowded aisle at Walmart, Darci's weight shifting to one foot and her forefinger tapping her chin as she stared at the pencil rack. She just didn't know whether to purchase plain yellow number twos with white erasers or the pack of mechanical ones with a vial of extra lead. She seemed to remember white erasers usually smudged the paper, and when you pushed the top of the mechanical ones, too much lead came out and broke off. Paxton endured all his nine-year-old patience could take, then let out an exasperated sigh. "For crying out loud, Mom. They're just pencils." He grabbed a pack hanging directly in front of him. "Here, these Batman ones are cool, problem solved." He pitched them in the shopping cart, then slapped himself in the forehead when Darci said they needed to pick out socks next, and asked if he'd rather get tubes or the ankle-length kind. Decisiveness was definitely not her strong point.

"Are y'all open on Thursdays, dear?" A woman Darci guessed to be in her early seventies set a Christmas cactus on the counter. "That's my shoppin' day, since the grocery store has double coupons on Thursday mornin'."

"Yes Ma'am. We'll be open Monday through Saturday all year, except Christmas Day." Darci fought the urge to do a little dance as she tapped the keys on the register to ring up the plant. "All other non-Sunday holidays, Petal Pushers will stay open at least until lunch."

Being the sole proprietor allowed Darci to set the schedule and make all the major decisions, and she planned to squeeze everything she could out of the next three hundred and sixty-five days. Sundays in a small town like Dixon, Kentucky, were pretty much devoid of shoppers, so there went fifty-two wasted days. Unless, of course, the only funeral parlor in town scheduled an after-church memorial service; then she'd stay open to fill last minute orders. Her being one of only two florists in the county sort of guaranteed she'd get at least half of all the local business. Next year she'd be able to afford to take more days off, but only after she proved to herself that she was capable of making this venture a success.

She sold three houseplants and two wreaths before noon, and gave away a good portion of her seed packets. Not bad for a day statistically ranked as the year's worst for sales.

The door bells sounded. Darci's stomach growled before she could look up to see Petal Pushers' next visitor. The smell of food always grabbed her attention.

"Bad as I hate to say it, I'm afraid you came to the wrong place. I didn't order anything. But I could use a takeout menu, though, if you've got one on you."

"Somebody ordered it for you." The delivery boy set two boxes of Chinese food on the counter before he handed her an envelope, then he reached in his jacket pocket for a menu. "Have a nice day."

She had the card out before the door closed behind him and read it as she ripped open the chopsticks.

To Darci on Opening Day,

I didn't know what to send to a florist, but I

figured this Szechuan chicken ought to hit your spot. I know John would've been so proud of you today, but since my best friend isn't here to tell you, I thought I'd do it for him.

Mae's coming in tomorrow but I don't want you to even think about giving her anything for free. Godparents are just like any other customers. Now don't bother to call and thank me or get all sentimental, just eat your damn food before it gets cold.

Love,
Max

Darci did as she was told and chowed down. She didn't want her baked goods to go to waste either, so she helped herself to a cruller for dessert. So much for her New Year's resolution to lose twenty pounds. She swiveled around in her chair, glanced at the door to make sure it wasn't ajar, then wondered where the cold draft was coming from. She made a mental note to have Wade check the seals around the windows and doors. The last thing she needed was a huge electric bill from running the heater full blast.

When the bell jingled later that afternoon, Darci beamed at the little guy who ran toward her.

"Hey Mom, how's it going?"

Before she could answer, Paxton spun her around and pulled her away from the door. "Cover your eyes. Dad and me bought you a surprise! You're gonna love it. Don't look yet." She heard Wade walk in behind her and set something on one of the tables. "Just one more second," Paxton said, bustling around. "Okay, now you can look."

Paxton and Wade flanked a square object the size of a small television. A big pink bow graced the towel that concealed whatever was underneath.

"What's this all about?"

"Since you've got the prettiest smile in town, I reckon we should give you a peek at your present." With a flourish, Wade whisked off the makeshift wrapping to reveal a parakeet currently too confused at her new surroundings to tweet. "You like it?"

Darci laughed as she bent down to take a closer look. "Thanks, I love it! What in the world made you two decide to buy me a bird? Of all things."

"We didn't want you to get lonely while you worked." Paxton's smile grew wider, obviously pleased his mother liked the parakeet he'd picked out. "She can keep you company."

Darci hugged both her guys. Paxton theatrically wiped off the kiss she planted on the tip of his nose.

"She'll be fun to have around, but you know I won't be alone here very often. I wasn't going to make anybody work on New Year's Day, but Charlotte will be here most mornings, working part-time now and after the baby's born."

"I still don't think she's really gonna have a baby." Paxton shook his head as he made what he must have thought was the obvious point. "She's skinny as a bean pole. When Jake's mom was gettin' ready to have his little brother, she got as big around as a hippopotamus."

Wade stifled a laugh with a fake cough as he and Darci exchanged an amused glance.

"Trust me, son, the doctor says you're gonna have a new baby cousin this July. Anyway, Charlotte called this morning to make sure I didn't need any help, which obviously," Darci motioned around the empty shop, "I didn't. And don't forget Hoyt comes in every afternoon to make deliveries and help with any heavy lifting we delicate girls can't handle."

She aimed the last comment at Paxton, who was going through a stage where he believed women couldn't lift anything heavier than a pie pan. His best friend Jake had put that idea in his head, thanks to his male chauvinist uncle.

"Hopefully he'll stick around through the summer to help with the landscaping jobs I'm sure you'll get." Wade smiled at her in that way of his that always set her heart aflutter. "When people get a load of all the plants and herbs and stuff you sell, you'll have to turn away customers to keep from sending the world into a flower

14

shortage."

"You're really gonna make the world run out of flowers?" Paxton exclaimed. "Cool."

"Not exactly, but I'm hoping to keep the greenhouse out back in constant need of restocking." The parakeet chirped and caught her attention. "I think I'll put her cage on the shelf hanging behind the counter so she can help me keep an eye on the customers."

"What're you gonna name her?" Paxton asked. "How about Hermione, like in *Harry Potter*?"

"Hmmm." Darci held the cage up to her face, scrutinizing the bird for ideas. "I don't know. Hermione just doesn't seem to fit her."

"Those dark green feathers on her back kind of match the flecks in your pretty brown eyes," Wade pointed out, his gaze causing an uncharacteristic blush to warm her cheeks. Since she didn't want Paxton to ask why her face was turning red, she focused on the parakeet.

"She's green, with a yellow head and wings, so she'll match most of the plants." She turned to face Wade and Paxton when the perfect moniker popped into her head. "I think I just might call her Daisy." Everyone agreed on the name as Darci set the cage in a prominent spot and made kissing noises at Daisy through the bars.

Before she closed up for the evening, Darci stood looking out what her son called the porthole, a circular window about two feet in diameter in the front right corner of the shop. She gazed through the side yard to the woods running behind it. The setting sun tinted the gray sky mauve, with blue highlights just above the distant trees. Bathed in the twilight glow that poured through the window, she hated to see this day end. Pulling on her coat, she glanced around her shop once more and headed for the door, still hardly able to believe she was actually living her dream.

Petal Pushers' Plant of the Month for January is

Nasturtium
Tropaeolum majus

Common Name: Indian Cress, Mexican Cress, and Peru Cress.

Brief description: These are one of the easiest flowers to grow from seeds, which makes them great for little kids or the green thumb challenged. The leaves look like little lily pads and the scented blooms come in orange, pink, yellow, red, and white. Nasturtiums grow about a foot tall, thrive in poor soil, and bloom from summer to fall.

Symbolism: Nasturtiums symbolize conquest, victory, and charity.

Trivia: This is an old flower that grew in ancient Rome.

Growing instructions: Plant seeds a half inch deep after the last spring frost in a place where they'll get a lot of sunshine. Deadhead wilted blooms.

Uses: These flowers are pretty in flowerbeds, borders, edgings, and window boxes. The edible blooms have a peppery taste, so use them in salads or as garnish.

Tools & Tips: Gardening gloves aren't just for the foo-foo who don't want to get dirt under their fingernails, even though they will help protect your manicure. Keep a few pairs handy year round to protect your hands when pulling weeds, pruning bushes, and spreading mulch.

A big THANK YOU to everybody who visited the shop in support of our Grand Opening. I'll update this Plant of the Month page each month, and you can usually find the profiled plant on sale, but for January, we're giving away nasturtium seeds. Please come in and get yours if you haven't already.

Chapter Two

February

The red rose whispers of passion,
And the white rose breathes of love;
O, the red rose is a falcon,
And the white rose is a dove.
~ John Boyle O'Reilly

"What do you think you're doing?" Darci tapped her foot as she glared at Charlotte, who sat working beside the helium tank.

"Blowing up balloons, Einstein. What's it look like?" Charlotte grinned up at Darci and offered her the nozzle. "Here, take a hit and say something funny."

"Don't think so." Darci twisted the knob to turn off the gas flow. "I'm not sure that's such a good idea. I'd never be able to forgive myself if that stuff . . . if it made you sick or anything." A few years back, Charlotte suffered through a miscarriage, a tragedy she refused to speak of, especially now, so Darci chose her words carefully.

"Shit, I didn't even think about that. I mean, it's just helium." Charlotte bit her lip while her hand swept protectively over her stomach.

"Oh, I'm sure you're fine, but just to be on the safe side, I'll do all the balloons for now," Darci said, trying to ease her cousin's worry. "While you're in the other room."

"Good idea. I don't want to have to name this kid Squeaky."

"We'll just move the tank to the kitchen so you don't forget. You ready for a lunch break?"

"Oh, please," Charlotte said, following her to the next room. "Like a pregnant woman would turn down food."

Charlotte fixed their drinks while Darci nuked two bowls of homemade soup in the microwave. The refrigerator stayed well stocked with food she whipped up in her spare time on Sunday afternoons. Darci liked cooking, but she enjoyed saving money even more.

The only extravagance she allowed herself while trying to make a success of her business was donuts from the Krispy Kreme down the street, and she limited that to twice a week.

Darci had put a pencil to food costs before she ever opened the store. Take-out lunch with a drink would cost at least seven bucks a day, which came to approximately forty-two dollars each six-day work week. No way in hell could she plunk down almost two hundred smackeroos a month just to eat it up and poop it out, not when every dime she spent took money out of Petal

Pushers' till. Everybody told her she was a good cook, and the homemade meals she brought in were a lot healthier for Paxton and Charlotte than french fries in a bag.

They sat down and Darci ladled up chunky chicken soup seasoned with herbs she'd grown herself the previous summer. "Smells good, even if I do say so myself." She noticed the green-tinged face across the table. "What's wrong?"

"Nothing. Looks yummy." Charlotte used her napkin to dab perspiration from her forehead, then stirred her soup. Beans and little pieces of celery swirled in the broth, bumping against chunks of roasted chicken breast. With her hand over her mouth and nose, she jumped up from her seat and ran to the bathroom.

Charlotte tried to apologize when she returned from tossing her cookies. "I'm sorry-"

"Don't worry about it," Darci cut her off with the wave of her hand, not in the least bit offended. "In a few weeks the morning sickness will be out of your system. Then you'll have, oh, maybe four months to eat whatever you want before the heartburn kicks in." A grin twitched on her lips and she just couldn't resist the next comment. "That's when the hemorrhoid fairy comes to visit."

"Oh, hell."

"Here, try to keep these down." She passed Charlotte a package of Ritz crackers.

The day before Valentine's Day, Paxton rode the school bus to his mom's store. He ate a sandwich and brownie as an afternoon snack and washed it down with a glass of milk in the kitchen. For a few minutes he seemed deep in thought, then scooted his chair over to where Darci sat filling Mylar balloons with helium.

"Um, what kind of stuff do people like to get for Valentine's Day?"

"You mean girl type people?"

"Well, yeah." He seemed consumed with the need to finish the last drop of milk, avoiding eye contact while he quenched his thirst.

Darci made sure the balloon she held blocked her expression from her son's view. One look at the stupid grin and he'd clam up for good. "A lot of guys order balloons for their girlfriends, and some girls like flowers or candy. And cards. Cards are always nice." She desperately tried not to look interested.

Paxton thought for a minute, seeming to ponder the idea. "So, would you like stuff like that? Balloons?"

"Sure I would. Tell you what. I'm going to make up some extra balloon bouquets as soon as I finish filling these orders. Pick out a few you might like to give your-" She faked a sneeze to stop herself from saying the dreaded 'g' word. Nine-year-old boys never wanted to admit to having a girlfriend. ". . . your friend, and I'll make a special one for you. Sound good?"

"Sounds great. Thanks, Mom."

Later, when she picked up the Mylar stack

Paxton left for her on the table, she couldn't wait to see which designs he chose. She carried them to the main room to show Charlotte.

"I think the boy has a little sweetheart." Darci beamed in the way only mothers can, when they think their child has just done the cutest thing ever. "Look at what he picked out, I'm guessing to take to the Valentine party at school tomorrow." She plopped three unfilled balloons down on the counter. The first two were a red one shaped like a heart and a round yellow happy face.

The last one caused Charlotte to ooh and ahh. "Oh, how cute! 'For my special girl'. Do we know who this mystery woman is?" Charlotte asked, her eyebrows wiggling maniacally up and down.

"I have absolutely no idea. Last I heard, he thought girls were icky and gross. About a week ago, he told Wade he'd eat a bug before he'd pick a girl to play on his team at recess." Darci shook her head. "It could even be his teacher, for all I know."

"So, let me guess. We're gonna stake out his fourth grade class under the pretense of delivering an emergency bouquet to the elementary school." Charlotte's laughter let Darci know she was joking, but that she wouldn't be at all surprised if their delivery van rolled up beside the school playground tomorrow.

"I'll see if he brings home any special valentines. And if that doesn't work," Darci narrowed her eyes into a conspiratorial glare, "I'll ply his best friend with Oreos and chocolate milk until he spills his guts."

23

Back at the helium tanks, Darci ran each of the female fourth graders' faces through her mind's eye, trying to figure out which one Paxton had a crush on. She leaned a bit towards Patsy Hoffman, a cute little redhead with green eyes and freckles on her nose. But somehow, she couldn't see her son infatuated with anyone who hadn't reached the third level of Galactasaur.

She finished the job by tying the balloon strings to a stuffed pink teddy bear, then sat it down by her purse so she wouldn't forget to take it home that night.

The parakeet was a wonderful diversion at the shop. Darci fed her treats and, within two weeks of having her, the little bird stepped onto her finger to come out of the cage. Whenever things got slow, Daisy rode on her shoulder, tweeting in her ear. The parakeet's clipped wings kept Darci from worrying about her flying out the door.

That afternoon, she was just about to put Daisy back in her cage when she felt goose bumps rise on her arms. "We're gonna have to get Wade to fix that before we freeze to death." Darci nuzzled the green and yellow bird, who chirped in agreement.

She covered the cage for the evening, then jumped at a noise to her right. A book about mosaic garden decorations had fallen off the shelf behind the counter. She put it back in its spot and tried to figure out why it tumbled down in the first place. The shelf didn't give when she tried to wiggle it.

The next morning she found the same book lying on the floor again. She took out a piece of stationary and made Wade a Honey-Do list: Number one, put more caulk or whatever you call it around the doors and windows to stop the drafts. Number two, level the bookshelf. Number three, a fresh box of donuts would really hit the spot. Hint, hint, pleeeze take the hint.

Got my eye on that Charlotte. I saw how she's a clutchin' at her belly and it just ain't right. I'll have to be doin' something about that directly.

Miss Darci has sure enough spiffied this place back up, all shinin' like a new copper penny, but she cain't take a hint to save her life. Might have to go upside her head with that big book to get my point across. Only one here I can communicate with is the little feather brain, for all the good that does. Oh me. If I get desperate, I reckon I can teach the bird to talk so she can just up and tell folks what I want. It's a miracle I managed to lure her here in the first place. But I did get her here, so surely to goodness I can figure out how to make her do the other things that need doin'. One way or the other.

At least I do know where it is now, but I cain't get a hold of it. Don't know who's to blame, but somebody's gonna have hell to pay for what they did, and I'll see things set right.

February fourteenth kept Petal Pushers bustling all day long. Charlotte came in for the morning shift and answered a dozen calls for last minute arrangements. Darci handled so many long-stemmed red roses, her fingers looked like something out of *The Mummy's Curse*. She'd misplaced the dethorner after lunch-she remembered fidgeting with the damn thing right before she made a ham and cheese sandwich, but she could *not* find it after dessert-and now Band-Aids covered her hands. Hoyt Simms, the high school senior who drove the delivery van as soon as the bell ended his biology class, burned up two tanks of gas hauling flowers all over the place, brightening the faces of Webster County's female residents.

Darci pulled into her own driveway that evening, exhausted from being on her feet all day but thrilled business was doing so well. Her mind wandered back to Paxton's 'special girl'. She wondered if he'd bring up the school Valentine party, though she doubted it. Asking point blank was certainly out of the question, since she figured he'd clam up and not mention another girlfriend until after his college graduation. Nope, she'd just have to wait it out . . . and pick up some extra Oreos before Jake's next visit.

"Hey, Hon. Pizza man's on his way," Wade yelled from the living room when she came through the front door.

"Great. My growling stomach was afraid you forgot to order it." She crossed the room to where he sat watching television and kissed him on the cheek.

"I'll get it," Paxton hollered when the doorbell rang. On his way to the door, he scooped up the bills Wade left on the table. "I know, I know. Two dollar tip."

Paxton liked paying for the pizza delivery, probably thinking it made him look like a responsible adult, or maybe it made him feel like a cool junior big shot. A few months before, he told the pizza guy to "Keep the change. Don't spend it all in one place," words Darci recognized from a movie they'd watched together. Ecstatic, the guy practically danced back to his car, pocketing the eighteen-dollar tip from a twenty-two dollar pepperoni and cheese pizza pie. Every time they ordered in after that, Wade and Darci reminded him at least twice while they waited for the knock at the door, "only two bucks, Rockefella".

The table was already set when Darci walked into the dining room. While she filled glasses with ice and Pepsi, Wade winked at Paxton, twitching his head toward the hall closet. He winked back as Wade guided Darci into her chair, then stood behind her with his hand over her eyes. Paxton's footsteps pattered back to the table. She heard something clink against her plate that didn't sound like crust and cheese. "Happy Valentine's Day, Mom!"

Wade uncovered her eyes. Darci saw what her guys had cooked up for her and beamed up at them both.

"This one's from Dad." Paxton pointed to a huge box of candy, her favorite mixed creams coated in dark chocolate. "And this one's from me." There, centered on her plate, sat a pink teddy bear holding the three balloons Darci tied to it yesterday. "Did you guess it was for you?"

After thanking them both, she answered his question. "It's a complete surprise! So I must be your special girl, huh, my sweet little pumpkin?"

"For cryin' out loud," Paxton crowed in a sarcastic little boy sort of way when she kissed him on his nose, but he was smiling at her. "You don't have to slobber all over me."

"Does this look okay?" Charlotte stepped back to scrutinize the funeral swag intended for the casket of one of Webster County's most prominent citizens. She'd spent the past two hours arranging blue carnations and baby's breath with a few different types of foliage. "I wasn't sure if I put in enough greenery to balance out the flowers."

"You did a great job, exactly what the Maldonado family requested," Darci said, very impressed after her perusal of her cousin's latest project. "Masculine, but pretty."

Before Charlotte came to work at Petal Pushers, she had no experience with floral design or even gardening, something no one would ever guess by looking at the beautiful arrangements she put together. She definitely had a flair for the job.

"Hoyt, if you could please load this swag into the van, I'll bring out the last memorial wreath. Then we need to get this stuff over to the funeral home." Darci added a blue ribbon to the oval and secured it in place through the Styrofoam base.

"No problem, Boss Lady," Hoyt said, a mischievous grin on his face. He ambled toward the back door, bobbing his head to the music from the earbuds connected to his iPod.

"You know I hate it when you call me that."

They took the delivery to the funeral home and had everything unloaded and set out before the viewing began.

Darci made it a policy to give her personal condolences at all the funerals where she delivered a large part of the flowers. Living in a small town like Dixon, she'd grown up acquainted with most of the residents and was related to more than half of the county's population. Darci wanted to make sure everyone knew that while her business was important to her, she valued her customers as individuals and friends, not just as people who helped her make her loan payments.

After she signed the visitor's register, Darci walked to the front of the funeral parlor and shook Mrs. Maldonado's hand. "So sorry for your loss." She never knew exactly what she should say, so that's the general condolence she usually went with. She cringed each time she heard the stupid line: 'Doesn't So-and-So look wonderful'. The deceased is dead, therefore he or she, in

Darci's humble opinion, undoubtedly looked a whole hell of a lot better when they were still alive. She'd often thought how insulted she'd be if she looked down from a cloud one day and heard people say she looked better dead than alive and kicking. Darci glanced at the coffin, then silently vowed to herself to find a way to haunt anybody who dared say that about her. As if that were possible.

Cyril Maldonado was fifty-three years old when he died on February twenty-second. His obituary described him as a veteran in the army, a life-long resident of Webster County, and survived by Pauline, his wife of thirty-one years, two grown children, and one grandchild. The obituary didn't say what Cyril died of, mainly because the cause of death had yet to be determined.

From listening to people who came through her shop to pick out funerary flowers, Darci had been able to fill in the circumstances surrounding Cyril Maldonado's death. Two days before he died, Cyril went to the Emergency Room complaining of vomiting and diarrhea. The admitting nurse noted that he suffered from severe dehydration and low blood pressure.

Cyril's friends told her that aside from a nasty case of chicken pox when his kids were in elementary school, he'd never really been sick. He might come down with an occasional cold, but he didn't have any preexisting conditions, no allergies, nothing that would explain his sudden onslaught of symptoms.

On Mr. Maldonado's second day in the hospital, the nurse buzzed the doctor when she noticed signs of internal bleeding. Confounded, the physician ran a new battery of tests. The results showed Maldonado's liver, spleen, and kidneys were shutting down. Cyril passed away later that afternoon.

Relatives, friends, war buddies, and associates of the gregarious Cyril Maldonado flooded the funeral home. His son and daughter flanked the new widow by the casket as she hugged a sobbing teenage girl with long dark hair. His sister and nephew flew in from Mississippi, no doubt having run into some of the men who went through boot camp with Cyril on their flight to say their final goodbyes.

Roy Nolan, Cyril's business partner and close friend, sat near the front, his dark eyes red and puffy. Grief made the thirty-one-year-old look much older than his years. The lady seated beside him with a cast on her arm, probably his mother, handed him a tissue and patted his knee when he clasped his hand over his eyes. By all accounts, Roy thought of Cyril not only as a buddy, but also a father figure. Eight years ago they'd opened M & N Stables, which bred some of the best thoroughbreds and quarter horses ever to graze on Kentucky bluegrass. They quickly became famous in the tri-state area for their expertise in equine training and therapy work, plus the extra care and attention they gave their clients kept the boarding stables filled to capacity.

On her drive back to the shop, Darci felt bad for Pauline Maldonado. Unable to picture her own life without Wade by her side, she could only imagine the depths of emotional turmoil the Maldonado family must be going through. At least she knew the widow was financially secure, since her husband left behind a large house and a successful business.

Wade treated the family to steak dinner and a movie on the last day of February, a tradition he'd started on January thirty-first. Proud of Darci for launching her business off with such a bang in the slowest retail season of the year, he planned to celebrate each milestone she hit along the way. His wife was hell bent on not only staying afloat this crucial first year, she'd set a goal of showing some type of profit by New Year's Eve. Self-employed most of his adult life, Wade knew all too well how challenging that would be.

She surprised him every step of the way with her determination and passion for the shop, and brought in more customers with her gimmicks and coupons than he would've dreamed possible. He'd known she had a flair for advertising ever since she woke up around two in the morning last November, unable to wait for sunrise to share her latest brilliant idea with him. He had to admit it was the ideal name, sure to stand out in people's minds when they needed flowers and plants.

"Petal Pushers! It's perfect. Get it?" He could see Darci's silhouette in the dark, her knees tucked underneath her as she sat beside him on the bed. She nudged his arm to keep him from falling back to sleep before he had a chance to jump for joy over her epiphany.

"Not really, but it sounds cute." He fluffed his pillow and turned onto his side, facing her. "I'm sure I'll love it in the morning." His lids fluttered to a close.

"No really, just think about it." She shook him back and forth by his arm more vigorously then, reminding him of his Aunt Eunice kneading bread dough. "Petal Pushers. We sell flowers, and when people think of florists, they picture flowers blooming. Which part do they visualize? The petals, of course, which sounds a lot more descriptive than just flowers."

"Great, Hon." Wade strained to keep his eyes open, afraid he'd get seasick if Darci didn't stop shaking him.

"Okay, now you see where I'm going," Darci tweeted faster than a hyper canary, focused on her store as she spoke. "We sell petals, so I thought petal shop, petal basket. . . no, too boring and ordinary. Then it hit me, woke me up from a sound sleep when it popped into my head. Pushing is another word for selling, like drug pushers sell dope, though I don't think anybody would confuse us with a bunch of junkies. Anyway, we push petals. Isn't that just the cutest name you ever heard for a flower store? Petal Pushers! Perfect."

"You're an advertising genius," Wade said, understanding why she was so excited. She'd thought up a shop name that would set her apart and people wouldn't be likely to forget. "Sounds like a winner."

"Shoot!" Darci set the clock back on the nightstand after holding it in front of her nose to see what time it was. "It's too late to call Charlotte."

Wade hid his grin in the pillow, wishing she would go ahead and share the joy with Charlotte anyway. She'd be more than happy to talk about it with her until the sun came up. Then maybe he could get some sleep.

Seated across from Darci now as he cut a piece from his rib-eye steak, he realized the only other time he'd seen her this happy was when Paxton was born. She'd loved fussing over him, which she still did, just without the diapers and formula. Darci was capable of just about anything when she set her mind to it. The fact that she managed to earn all the startup money proved that. They'd argued quite a bit when she refused to let him help finance the place, but she finally convinced him it was something she needed to do for herself, to prove she could be independent even if she didn't need to be. There wasn't a doubt in his mind that Petal Pushers would be the most successful flower shop in the state. Darci was amazing.

Petal Pushers' Plant of the Month for February is

The Knock Out Rose
Rosa x
Deciduous shrub

Brief description: This is the easiest rose to grow, and one of the most beautiful. Available in a variety of colors, it blooms non-stop from late spring until frost. They grow to about three or four feet in height and width, and have a light fragrance.

Symbolism: Roses have a language of their own, based on their color:

Red roses symbolize love, romance, respect, perfection, beauty, and congratulations.

Yellow roses mean friendship, warmth, happiness, a new beginning, and remembrance.

White roses stand for innocence, purity, girlhood, and honor.

Pink roses are a symbol of grace, elegance, thanks, appreciation, and admiration.

Orange roses mean passion, fascination, excitement, desire, and enthusiasm.

Lavender roses are a sign of enchantment and love at first sight.

Black roses, well, these usually mean somebody is out to get you . . . in a bad way.

Trivia: Rose breeder William Radler developed Knock Out roses in 1988, making it possible for just about everybody to grow these gorgeous flowers.

Growing instructions: Plant in full sun to partial shade, then watch them grow and bloom. These roses are disease resistant and don't even need to be deadheaded. Your neighbors will think you have a green thumb when they see these in your yard. Take them a bouquet to be nice (and make them jealous).

Uses: Knock Out Roses are beautiful just about anywhere outside.

Tools & Tips: Roses are much more romantic if the hand that holds them isn't bleeding. Buy yourself a rose dethorner if you grow your own bouquets. This little gadget is easy to use, and gets rid of those thorns and leaves in one easy motion.

Chapter Three

March

Flowers are the sweetest things God
ever made and forgot to put a soul into.
~ Henry Ward Beecher

"Careful with those ferns, Hoyt," Darci said, picking up a box loaded down with centerpieces. "Don't get the fronds caught in the door."

She viewed this wedding as her public debut, the biggest shindig to take place in the county so far this year, an event with pews full of potential customers who would, with any luck, drool over the floral decorations which had been the center of her existence for the past two weeks. Celia Kemp, the society columnist for the local newspaper, should be getting her butt to the church pretty soon, lest she not have enough time to snoop around looking for imperfections in, well, everything.

Darci, Charlotte, and Hoyt bustled around the First Baptist church all morning, making things pristine for the Blanford-Frye wedding. The bridesmaids' flowers and groomsmen's boutonnieres now adorned the respective hands and lapels, a basket of assorted petals awaited the flower girl, greenery and roses bedecked the altar, and since Hoyt was on his way to place massive ferns on their pedestals on both sides of the pulpit, their work was nearly done.

Centerpieces soon graced each table in the reception room next door. Darci helped herself to a palmful of mixed nuts and a couple mints as she passed the buffet. Charlotte looked like she was going to barf when she offered her a cashew, so Darci didn't waste any time getting her back outside for some fresh air. Puke would definitely clash with the décor.

The bride's mother had burst into tears when Charlotte handed her the bridal bouquet, a beautiful combination of lilies and pink rosebuds. Apparently, breaking down in sobs wasn't all that unusual for Mrs. Blanford, since her husband seemed to be expecting it. With a little white nerve pill proffered in his hand, he stepped up and put his arm around her. "There, there, Blanche. You don't want to go and mess up your makeup with all that cryin'." He winked at Darci and Charlotte as he led his wife to the water fountain.

Darci slipped her feet out of her comfortable loafers and squeezed them into more fashionable black pumps, then checked her appearance in the delivery van's rearview mirror. Charlotte and Hoyt weren't sticking around for the nuptials, but, since the groom's parents personally asked Darci to stay, how could she refuse? The Frye's cousin was a good friend of her mother's, after all, making them nearly an acquaintance. Small-town connections run even deeper than Six Degrees to Kevin Bacon, the game where every Hollywood personality can be linked to the Footloose star by association.

Her employees left in Charlotte's car, Hoyt blasting Godsmack as they spun out of the driveway. Darci headed back inside the church, which had steadily filled with friends and loved ones of the wedding party. She took a seat on the back pew on the groom's side. A few minutes later, a woman slipped in and hurried to sit down on the end near Darci. The late arrival seemed very nervous, biting her nails and shifting her weight from one butt cheek to the other on the hard wooden bench.

Piano music beckoned the bridesmaids to get the show on the road. Each carried one perfect white calla lily tied with lace ribbon that matched their shell pink gowns. The cutest little five-year-old flower girl followed, scattering petals over the walkway; she paused once to throw a handful at her uncle, which elicited chuckles from the onlookers. Everyone stood for the wedding march while the father of the bride walked his daughter down the aisle. After he raised her veil and answered the customary "Who gives this woman" question, he took his seat beside his wife, a drug induced dilation visible in her puffy red eyes.

Darci scanned her handiwork, which decorated the bride and groom as well as the church, pleased with the simple elegance of the lilies and pink roses against the greenery. She tried not to let her head swell when she overheard people around her rave about the flowers.

A glance toward the minister showed the ring ceremony was underway. The handbag fell off the lap of the woman seated beside her, who quickly picked it up and clutched the handle in her sweaty fist. Darci almost offered her a cough drop when the woman cleared her throat, but wasn't sure if she had any in her purse.

"If anyone present has just cause why this couple should not be united in the bonds of holy matrimony, let them speak now or-"

"I can't hold my tongue any longer."

A collective gasp echoed through the house of worship, then all fell silent. Everyone turned to face the nervous woman who stood to interrupt the preacher man.

"Preacher, you need to take a few steps back from that little Jezebel," she said, moving into the aisle. Her hands shook as she swallowed hard, attempting to keep her composure. "I'm afraid you might get struck by a stray lightning bolt any second."

"What's the meaning of this?" The reverend's befuddled expression made it clear this sort of thing didn't usually happen. "Why don't you sit back down and-"

A few people moved as if to approach her, but

her next words stopped them in their tracks.

"That slut is bonking my husband." Her voice shook with indignation. "They've been going at it in the Dew Drop Motel on Highway 41-A for the past couple of months, maybe longer."

The bride took a step toward her fiancé. Her wide eyes threatened to take over her face, which grew paler with each passing second. "I don't know what that crazy bitch is talking about." Her expletive shocked a few older parishioners on the third pew.

The bridesmaids exchanged worried glances with each other, whispering behind their calla lilies as Mrs. Blanford wailed. The groomsmen grinned like idiots.

Darci hated to see the wedding fall to ruin, not just because she'd put so much work into it herself, but because she felt sorry for the young couple who stood at the altar. She felt bad for them, but she wouldn't have traded her seat with anybody, since she had the best view of the woman causing all the trouble.

"So now I'm crazy? It's not bad enough you've been playing hide the salami with Morty, now you call me crazy!" Rage tinged her cheeks red as she reached into her handbag and withdrew an envelope of six-by-four-inch photographs. "This will show you and everybody else who *isn't* crazy exactly who *is* a slut. That would be you." She promptly took out the pictures and let the envelope flutter to the ground at her feet. Armed with extra copies which she passed out to the crowd, she saved two particularly interesting ones for

Matthew Frye. It wasn't exactly the wedding gift he'd hoped for.

Judging by the disgust that twisted his face, he most likely held the twins to the photos Darci'd been passed. She was amazed the place hadn't gone up in flames like the gym in *Carrie*, positive this sort of pornographic color glossies had never before polluted this conservative Baptist church.

The first one showed a profile of the bride-to-be performing fellatio on a middle-aged man assumed to be Morty, the indignant lady's husband. Seated in an office chair, ole Morty's grotesquely jubilant expression suggested he was either enjoying the hell out of himself or in the throes of some type of seizure. Hard as it was to tear her eyes from that proverbial train wreck, she couldn't wait to see what the next photo showed.

It was even worse. The couple sprawled across a couch, both totally naked but for a pair of black socks on his feet. Morty groped Belinda's ta-tas, which she looked to be enjoying. Their pastime of choice was obvious. On her back, one knee jutted up on either side of Morty's ass, his cheeks the same shade of white as the calla lilies the bridesmaids held now.

A scream came from the front row, and Darci guessed the mother of the bride had seen the photos.

"Belinda Elizabeth Blanford, what in the name of God is wrong with you?" Mrs. Blanford shrieked as her husband held her up by her elbow. Silence gripped her momentarily as she searched for a way to rationalize the situation and-for the sake of saving face in a community where everybody knew everything that went on-found a way to place the blame on anyone except her daughter. "Did that man take advantage of you, baby?"

"Ha, take advantage of *her*! I knew this was a bad idea the first time my son brought your trollop daughter through my front door." Apparently, a set of the photographs had also fallen into the hands of Mrs. Frye, mother of the groom. "The whole town knows she acts like gutter trash, but good lord, I didn't think she'd stoop to *this*, and with some old geezer. My poor, poor boy, falling for somebody who gets poked more than a pincushion." She headed toward the altar to console her heartbroken son.

"Don't you dare talk that way about Belinda." Mr. Blanford plopped his inconsolable wife down onto the pew and blocked Mrs. Frye's way. "Any yahoo in the country could have very easily doctored those pictures in Photoshop."

Now Mr. Frye, father of the groom, stepped between his wife and his son's would be father-in-law. "Don't use that tone with my wife. You need to be giving your daughter a good talkin' to, is what you need to do. If she'd been raised right, she wouldn't be out lifting her skirt to every Tom, Dick, and Morty who crosses her path."

"Hold it right there," said Mrs. Morty. She dipped her hand back into her purse to withdraw another envelope. "The private investigator I hired to follow Morty was kind enough to start tailing Matthew, after we found out what was going on between that whore Belinda and my husband, plus a few other guys he caught her out fornicating with. Since she didn't care about breaking my heart by screwing up my marriage, I thought I should return the favor."

Whispers of speculation rippled through the crowded pews. One of the groomsmen pulled a small silver flask from his coat pocket, took a swig, then passed it around to the other young men standing beside him. Darci thought she might like a draw, herself. This was certainly the most exciting wedding she'd ever attended.

"These pictures show Matthew isn't such a high and mighty young man, himself. Oh, and I have the negatives, if anybody needs proof they weren't tampered with. Anyway," she said, pulling the pictures out one at a time before passing them through the crowd as she'd done with the first set. "These show Matthew going at it with some blonde floozy . . . . Funny, she seems to look sort of familiar." Cocking her head, she shifted her gaze to the bridal party and pointed a finger at the woman standing to the bride's left. "I guess Matthew has been schtupping the maid of honor."

"Kaylee, you whore!" Belinda pivoted around and slapped the blonde in question across the face, jumping at the chance to turn from being the accused to the accuser. Behind her, the best man elbowed Matthew, shooting him a quizzical look that made it apparent this was all news to

46

him. Matthew said something into his ear that made the groomsmen laugh. The high five they exchanged thoroughly pissed off the bride's father, who stormed up to the altar and began a heated argument with them.

Kaylee decided the best thing to do in this unexpected situation was to get the hell out of Dodge. She threw down her calla lily, hefted up her long skirt, and ran bawling back down the aisle and through the front door. Darci had never seen anyone run like that in high heels, and wondered whether Kaylee got in her car or just kept right on running until she reached her house. The bridesmaid's stiletto sprint ought to be an Olympic event, she thought, then turned her attention back to the chaos still unfolding.

Mrs. Frye fainted after seeing the photo of her son Matthew tangled up in the backseat of the family Buick with Kaylee Peters. The irony of the girl's last name didn't seem to be lost on anyone, judging by the raunchy comments drifting through the crowd. The Frye's ten-year-old daughter ran to fetch a cup of water from the fountain. On returning, she stood confused as to what she should do next. She opted for splashing the contents of the Dixie Cup into her mom's face. Mrs. Frye sat up sputtering and gasping for air, choking on the water that sloshed up her nose.

Just when it looked like things couldn't possibly get any worse, they did. People seated on the front rows murmured and looked from the front of the beautifully decorated church to the bride and groom, then to the lady Darci now thought of as Mrs. Morty. From out of one of the Sunday school classrooms walked a man everyone knew from the pictures, though he would have been recognized even quicker if he'd taken off his pants and walked in butt first. He staggered in slurring declarations of love to Belinda. Darci assumed Morty'd been hitting the hootch.

Slobbering all over himself, Morty fell to his knees in front of the blushing bride. He hugged her around the legs as he sobbed into the fluffy cloud of tulle-embellished skirt. "Come on, sugar. Don't marry that dumb sombitch. He's no good for you." No one thought to turn off the microphone used during the ceremony so Morty's drunken pleas echoed loudly through the church. "We can run away to Mexico or Tahiti or any other damn tropical place where nobody'll find us. You know you're my one and only, Sugar Feet. I love you so much! We can get married, and buy a dog, and-"

Morty's wife plucked a hymnal from its receptacle on the back of a pew, then whacked Morty a couple of good licks over his head with it. The preacher caught the book on its downward arc just in time to stop it from breaking Belinda's nose.

"Lord have mercy on us all," the reverend exclaimed, restraining Mrs. Morty in a bear hug around her arms and body. She continued to lunge toward her husband, shouting profanity the likes of which had never been heard inside the little Baptist church.

Matthew and Mr. Blanford shoved each other back and forth while the mothers of the bride and groom shouted in each other's faces, defending their child while pointing out the lack of moral fiber in the other. Mr. Frye took his younger daughter outside to their car, which he drove to the front steps so his son could make a fast get-away. As he made his way back inside and toward his son, the minister spoke again, this time becoming a bit exasperated and losing his composure.

"Come on people, get a hold of yourselves! This is the House of God, not Friday night mud wrestling over at Babes-a-rama." He turned to address the larger group of people gaping at all the commotion. "Could some of y'all find it in your hearts to help me get these folks away from each other and out of here before somebody has to call the law?"

As people moved forward to assist, Darci thought it was a good time to leave. She ebbed along among a wave of others with the same idea, all of whom kept glancing back over their shoulders until they were out of sight of all the action.

The Blanford-Frye wedding fiasco was the talk of the town for weeks afterward.

"Damn! You would know I'd leave before all the excitement started." Charlotte couldn't believe she missed the event of the century. At least she got a firsthand account of the chaos from Darci.

Surprisingly enough, after people got the gossip out of the way, they raved about the floral arrangements. Darci booked two more weddings

before the week was out, and Petal Pushers enjoyed an increased number of first time customers. Three-fourths of them pumped her for more
information on the Morty affair, and everybody
left with a plant, cut flowers, or an arrangement
in hand.

When Darci opened the store on Saint Patrick's Day, she came prepared for nothing out of
the ordinary. It wasn't a big holiday in the florist
business, but she hoped to sell a few things she'd
advertised in that week's fliers. Designed to ward
off pinches due to lack of green attire on the sev-
enteenth, a box full of St. Patrick's Day buttons
with little leprechauns dancing on a field of green
sat on the counter. The flier featured a coupon
for a dollar off *Oxalis deppei*, better known as
shamrock plants. The green and purple houseplants filled the display table in the center of the
room, their clover-like leaves festive beneath delicate pink blooms.

"Well, would you look at this." Darci picked up
a potted spider plant from the stool by the porthole window, then held it out to Charlotte. "What
do you think? Luck of the Irish, maybe?"

The previous afternoon, a customer returned
the plant because its leaves had started to dry up
and fall off. It was pretty obvious to Darci and
Charlotte that it hadn't seen a drop of water in at
least a week. Rather than point out the obvious,
Darci took the plant back and talked Mrs. Jen-

kins into a jade plant instead, a hardy dark green succulent which could thrive in a drought. She didn't mention that detail to the now happy Mrs. Jenkins, afraid that if she did, the lady would restrict herself to watering it once a month.

The spider plant Charlotte gaped at this morning seemed to be the picture of health, ready for a photo shoot in *Better Homes and Gardens*.

"Freaky. If we hadn't walked in here at the same time, I would've sworn you were trying to get one over on the pregnant girl. This *is* the same plant, right?" Charlotte wore an expression of amused confusion.

"Yep, definitely the same plant. Don't think anybody would have broken in to switch out the stock and leave the till in the cash register." Darci squinted at the pot, then stuck her finger in the dirt, testing the moisture as she examined the soil particles stuck to her index finger. "Did you fertilize it when you watered it?"

"Nope, just H2O straight out of the tap."

"Hell if I know." Darci shook her head. "Maybe we have some weird magical draft blowing through here or something. It's worse there by the porthole and over by the counter. Wade came in last Saturday, when it was so windy, and went over the windows and door seals, but he couldn't find where the air was coming in."

"Weird."

At the end of the month, Darci balanced the books, thrilled to find their profit margin growing steadily wider with each passing week. They still had a ways to go before she could declare the business a success, but at least now she was a little more confident she was doing something right.

She always went over the financial stuff three times, just to make sure she caught all her mistakes. Darci sucked at math and she knew it. How she ever passed her college algebra class was beyond her. Maybe Professor Tannenbaum thought she was cute, or maybe he just passed everybody to make himself look like a wonderful teacher. He had won 'Teacher of the Year' that semester, if she remembered correctly. Oh well, she guessed it really didn't matter now. She *did* know how to add and subtract-so long as her calculator batteries didn't go flat-and could tell the difference between positive numbers, which gave her a rush like biting into a chocolate éclair, and negative numbers, which meant growing debt and made her feel stupid. For now, she was starting to use the black ink pen more than the red one.

For the moment, at least, it looked as if she might actually be able to make her business a success. With a smile, she snapped the ledger closed, then turned to give Daisy a fresh sprig of millet. "So far, so good, my little feathered buddy."

Petal Pushers' Plant of the Month for March is

Shamrock Plant
Oxalis deppei
Perennial Bulb

Common name: Good Luck Plant, Iron Cross, False Shamrock, and Lucky Clover.

Brief description: This plant really is made up of four-leaf clovers, but unlike the ones you might find in your yard, the centers of these are purple. Pink blooms appear in summer, but the foliage makes this an attractive plant year round.

Symbolism: good luck.

Trivia: This native of Mexico became popular with plant collectors during the Victorian era.

Growing instructions: These plants like moist soil and bright indirect light. They reach ten to twelve inches tall. Plant the bulbs two inches deep, and they'll bloom in twelve weeks. When your shamrock plant starts to look puny, let it have a dormant period for a few months, then start watering it again and it should perk right up.

Uses: These shamrock plants are good in containers indoors, but can be planted outside. They are perfect for window boxes.

Tools & Tips: March is the time to start your seedlings, so they'll be ready to set out after the last frost. You can buy seed starter kits with plastic lids, or just use paper cups or egg cartons that you fill with potting soil. Add your seeds of choice, water, and cover with plastic wrap. Place whichever you decide to use in a sunny window, keep the soil moist, and remove the plastic cover or wrap whenever the seedlings start to grow.

In honor of St. Patrick's Day, Greta Greeley has set up a beautiful display at the Webster County library, with shamrock plants and ceramic Leprechauns. Stop by and have a look sometime this month.

Chapter Four

April

*I perhaps owe having become a painter
to flowers.*
~ Claude Monet

"Whatcha working on?" Darci walked behind the counter, curious to see what had her cousin so intrigued in the internet. Charlotte's short blonde curls were as tidy as ever, though her roots were getting darker by the day. Unable to bleach it the 'natural' shade it'd been for the past ten years, her hairdresser had to use non-chemical colorants during the pregnancy.

"Baby names. Jimbo and me can't agree on anything, except that we both hate the names Gertrude and Peter." Charlotte scrolled down a page full of the top five hundred names for babies, the meanings and country where the name originated listed to the right of each.

"It would save fifty percent of the headache if

you'd just let the doctor tell you whether it's going to be a boy or a girl." Darci bent closer to get a glimpse at the monitor, unable to stop herself from tousling the blonde hair beside her. "Your roots are showing."

"Thanks for pointing that out." She coughed and said "bitch" at the same time, which caused them both to laugh. Charlotte took her hand off the mouse halfway through the 'T' names for girls. "How about Turquoise? That's pretty, and you don't hear it too much. And Twyla, that's kinda cute. What do you think?"

"Um, to be honest," Darci said, the corners of her lips turned up in a sarcastic grin, "I think your mom is going to shit tulips if you name her grandbaby Turquoise Twyla. Sounds like a stripper from the eighteen-hundreds."

"You're probably right. Still a cute name, though." Charlotte tapped the mouse to bring up boy names that started with 'F'. "Okay, let's see what we have here. Farouk, Festus, and Filbert, like the nut. Well, I guess if it's a boy, his first initial definitely won't be 'F'."

"You could always do what our folks did and name the kid after his grandparents," Darci suggested, trying to help.

"That worked out so well for us, didn't it? Darci Odette Shelton."

"I don't know, Charlotte Louise Villines, you tell me." Darci dodged a wadded up piece of notepaper Charlotte pitched at her head. "Don't stress about it. You still have three whole months before you're due. You'll think of something. Just don't go with the antique stripper names. How've you been feeling? You look perkier since you put the morning sickness behind you."

"My appetite is fine, as you can tell, since I've gained thirty-two pounds already. Flip-flops are the only kind of shoe that fits on my big fat swollen feet, and even though I'm exhausted all the time, it's hard to sleep because the kid's foot or head or something is stuck in my ribs twenty-four seven." She reminded Darci of their Aunt Faith, the woman who was never happier than when she recited her laundry list of ailments. "And, to top all that loveliness off, I think I'm starting to hallucinate."

"You're seeing things? Like what?" Darci looked at her skeptically, sure she was about to hear a joke. "Giant pickles covered in peanut butter throwing themselves down your throat?"

"Shut up. I only ate that once. Okay, twice, but it tastes so much better than it sounds. Anyway, when I came back in here from my tenth bathroom break of the day, I could've sworn I saw an older lady standing over there, looking out the porthole." Charlotte bit her lip, which let Darci know there would be no punch line.

"So, what did she look like?"

"I don't know, like she was from some religious cult or something. Her hair was piled on her head and she wore a long dark outfit. I only saw her for a second before I realized it was a hallucination, 'cuz then I was staring at empty air."

"Don't worry about it, you're probably just tired. The sun could have been playing tricks on you, or maybe it was just shadows from the trees blowing in the wind outside."

"I'm not worried, just thought it was weird." Charlotte did look relaxed, though she was staring toward the kitchen just then. "Do we have any peanut butter . . . or dill pickles?"

Creeping around under the full moon yesterday evenin' sure did me a world of good. Been havin' a ball puttin' my green thumb to work again, and it sure enough is fun to see the look on the girls' faces when they take a gander at the plants I nurse back to health in the parlor, but it doesn't compare to being back out and about. Located the cramp bark easy enough down the street but I like to never found that dang false unicorn root. Had to dig around in the woods by Slover Creek, but I got me a good little bit of it.

Whatever's happened to me makes it slow goin' packin' stuff around. I swan, took me half the night to bring those herbs back here, and longer than that to grind 'em up real fine. Glad to have that over with. Aint' nothing a 'tall to mixin' it in Charlotte's tea, and it ought to take a hold on that baby she's carryin' any time now. It's still hard to communicate with these people, but I can make her see me for a few seconds now. While she's lookin' for where I disappear to, I sprinkle the powdered herbs in the raspberry tea I got her hooked on a while back.

I'm so close to getting my hands on my delicate

little treasure, I just have to get it out.

The following week, Sheriff Maxwell Roberts stopped by Petal Pushers to buy a rose bush and a pretty bouquet for his wife's birthday. Darci told her godfather to follow her back to the work-room to help select the flowers.

"So how've you been doing, Max?" Nearly everybody called him Max. When people needed him in a professional capacity, then he was Sheriff. The only person who addressed him as Maxwell was his wife, but only when he'd done something to put himself in the doghouse.

"The Maldonado case has been keeping me pretty busy, here lately," he said.

"Really? I knew his death was unexpected and had the doctors stumped, but I didn't know there was an investigation going on." Darci ran her hand over containers of fresh flowers until her palm slowed to hover above in-season daffodils. "You like these?"

"Perfect, Mae loves Easter flowers. Could you mix in a few red roses, maybe?"

"For a law man, you've got great taste in floral design." Darci grinned at him. Most men couldn't tell ivy from hydrangeas, so it was a nice change of pace to have a customer who actually knew what kind of flowers his wife liked, and what looked nice together. Her fingers danced over the forest of blooms again before she withdrew the perfect thing. "These red buds should do the trick. They'll open up over the next few days and last even after the daffodils start to droop. Yep, you've got great taste, Max."

"Mae trained me pretty well."

"So, is the Maldonado case confidential or can you talk about it?" Darci went to work arranging the bouquet. She added a couple fern fronds and some filler with tiny purple blossoms. "Not being nosey, just curious."

"It's no big secret. And every damn body I talk to is pretty curious about it." Max chuckled. There weren't many secrets in a small town. "The autopsy came back showing poison in his system. Something called ricin. Thing is, we can't figure out how he came to ingest it."

"What is ricin? Some kind of chemical?"

"Well, sort of. It's found in all types of stuff. Castor oil, wood and leather preservatives, lubricants, and some cosmetics." A master of deadpanning, Max couldn't pass up a wise crack, not even about this case. "We can probably rule out the makeup. Far as I know, ole Cyril wasn't a transvestite."

"No." Darci shot him a look over the worktable. "I'd think his army buddies would've remembered if he showed up to boot camp in his wife's bra and panties."

"Franny, the receptionist over at M & N Stables, couldn't think of anything out of the ordinary. Cyril and Roy hadn't ordered any new horse medications, there hadn't been any construction going on, and Cyril didn't show up wearing blusher." He winked at Darci. "They ate in the office, as usual, taking turns picking up plate lunches from the restaurant downtown. That's where I'm heading next. 'Bout to starve, so a plate of their beans, greens, and cornbread ought to hit the spot. Nobody else in town got sick like that, so I think it's safe to say their food isn't tainted."

Darci heated up her own lunch after he left. Charlotte had the day off for a doctor's appointment-Braxton Hicks contractions had been bothering the poor thing, the false labor pains troubling her more than she'd let on-so Darci ate her tomato soup and grilled cheese alone, listening to Daisy chirp in the next room. Her thoughts kept drifting back to her conversation with Max. Why did ricin sound familiar? Probably just a word she'd heard on some talk show or documentary about poison, she guessed.

She dismissed it and shifted her thoughts to her Earth Day promotion, trying to decide whether or not 'Buy a plant, save the planet' was politically correct or just plain pushy. Green Earth Day balloons filled with helium danced in her imagination. Instead of the Mylar ones the shop usually used, these would be the plain ole latex kind, the slogan 'Petal Pushers First Annual Earth Day Celebration' emblazoned across them in pale yellow lettering. The freebies should bring in quite a few people, most of whom would feel cheap if they didn't buy something before they left with a gratis balloon floating over their child's head.

Daisy chirped happily as she climbed her new bird gym on the shelf next to her cage. This parakeet playground behind the counter quickly became popular with patrons who strolled through the store.

Darci helped a customer with a selection of centerpieces. He wanted an arrangement for his anniversary and clearly showed a preference for cut flowers and elegant crystal candleholders.

"This one is perfect!" He held it up to the window, which caused the delicate prisms to cast rainbows across his face and the wall behind him. "If it's not too much trouble, could you add a few sprigs of rosemary? It symbolizes remembrance, I think, and I want us to remember the special times we've had since we've been together."

"This'll add a nice fragrance, too," Darci said moments later when she came back from the next room where she kept a supply of fresh herbs, something always in demand during the growing season. "How long have you and your wife been married?"

The man opened his mouth to say something, then paused for a second as if shifting the direction of his thoughts. "This is our sixth anniversary." His face lit up in a way that let Darci know he must still be very much in love.

She rang up the sale after muffling the centerpiece-an elegant grouping of seasonal hyacinths, double orange tulips, and now rosemary sprigs-in tissue paper inside a sturdy green cardboard box.

Can we trade a few business cards?" He reached into his pocket for a small case. "I have a hair salon in Lisman. We opened last fall and I'm always looking for new clients."

"Sure." Glad to exchange some of her extra business cards for his, she read the top one as she placed his stack beside the register. Hair Dare Your 'Do Salon, Donovan Lewis, proprietor and master stylist. "Think you could do anything to glam up my wash and wear do?"

Darci twirled a mousy brown strand around her index finger, wishing she'd taken the time to hit it with a styling tool this morning before she came to work.

"Your hair is just lovely. Hmmmm." Donovan tapped his chin a few times, the better to study what Darci figured must look like a rat's nest piled on her head. "We could add some layers, oh, and maybe some caramel highlights."

"Are y'all open on Sundays?" Sunday was her only day off. The thought of taking time away from the flower shop for herself, even a few minutes for a quick trim, made her queasy.

"Yes we are, from noon til four," Donovan answered proudly.

"Great. Then I'll call this afternoon and set up an appointment." Darci slid his parcel across the counter. "And happy anniversary. I hope she likes the centerpiece."

"Thank you. I'm certain it will be very much appreciated."

The only thing that brightened her day more

than a happy customer was one who promised to spread the word about Petal Pushers.

The door jingled behind him as he walked down to the street to the home he shared with Bradley. He'd come very close to telling the shopkeeper about the nature of his relationship, but decided against it at the last minute. If she wasn't accepting of their lifestyle, he didn't want it to put a damper on the special night he had planned.

Donovan carefully removed the beautiful arrangement from the box and placed it in the center of the cherry dining table, already set with Limoges china and crystal stemware. The silverware Bradley's aunt gave them after their civil ceremony sparkled against the linen napkins. He stood back to admire the table, then went to the kitchen to start cooking dinner.

With the Cornish hens seasoned and snugly roasting in the oven surrounded by glazed carrots, he went to work on the risotto.

He heard a knock and the backdoor creak open, sounds that meant his best friend had stopped to visit. "Come on in, Gwen."

"Hey, something smells good." Gwen sniffed again, looking around for something to sample. She set the bottle she carried on the bar and popped a stray chunk of carrot in her mouth. "There's the booze you asked me to pick up."

"Thanks for saving me a trip." Donovan gave

Gwen a quick peck on the cheek, put the champagne in the refrigerator to chill, then went back to stirring his risotto.

"No problem, and happy anniversary. Are any of y'all's relatives coming down to help you celebrate?"

"You know that's not very likely." Donovan put the lid on the simmering pot and aimed a smile toward his guest. When Donovan came out of the closet at twenty-one, his conservative family disowned him. He kept in contact with his grandmother and younger brother, but to the rest of his family, he might as well be dead or living on Mars. "Grandmother did send us a lovely card, though."

"I thought Bradley's brother or sister might be coming."

"No, we're just going to have a cozy evening for two. Food, bubbly, and my honey."

Bradley's family accepted his orientation from the beginning. His mother had an idea about his sexuality when he preferred to play with his sister's Barbies rather than his big brother's football gear. Bradley expected his parents and siblings to embrace Donovan the same way they had his former boyfriends, though there hadn't been many others.

When Bradley brought Donovan to Sunday dinner at his parents' home about a week after they moved in together, they weren't prepared for the icy reception. While accepting the nature of their relationship, the Slatons were less than thrilled with Donovan's white complexion.

Bradley had gone over alone the following day to get to the bottom of the matter. His family said Donovan seemed like a nice enough guy, but they preferred to see Bradley with someone of his own race. Somehow, Bradley had never given much thought to his parents' views on mixed couples, since they had many Caucasian friends and associates. His previous boyfriends had been black-well, one was a dark skinned Latino, but in retrospect, that probably seemed close enough for the Slatons.

Crushed, Bradley confided the problem to Donovan. Since he'd been shunned by his own family, he thought it was promising that Bradley's parents said they were willing to try to get over their aversions to the relationship. Bradley felt the strain more as time went on, until finally the couple decided to relocate to a place where neither of them knew a soul and start a new life together.

An up-and-coming young architect, Bradley soon received positive responses to the resumes he sent out. He took a job with a company in Evansville, Indiana. He and Donovan scouted the area for a nice place to live and on a whim ventured across the bridge to look in smaller Kentucky towns. When the realtor showed them a cottage with beige siding and blue shutters, they decided to call it home.

"That sounds perfect and romantic," Gwen said, helping herself to some of Donovan's homemade coffeecake. He kept his fresh baked goodies on the counter, and she never missed an opportunity to let him know she enjoyed his cooking. "Mmmm. Delicious. Do you ever regret moving here? I know Dixon is a far cry from Chicago and St. Louis."

"No, we love it here," Donovan smiled, passing Gwen a napkin, "but we did wonder how residents in this small Southern community would react to a mixed gay couple in their neighborhood." Fortunately, most of the people in Webster County were congenial and tolerant. The couple from next door didn't bat an eye when they brought over a Bundt cake to welcome them to Dixon. Word did get around that they were a different sort of couple, but nobody caused any real trouble for them. "Now that the theatrics with Nelson are over, we wouldn't want to live anywhere else."

The redneck across the street was their sole antagonist. Todd Nelson would wave flamboyantly to them when they were in the front yard, his pinky finger extended like Mr. Roper from the old *Three's Company* sitcom. He used the couple across the street as entertainment when his drinking buddies came over. At least they viewed them as a comical distraction and didn't try to beat them up, unlike gay bashers Donovan had encountered in his Missouri hometown. Still, he didn't appreciate the nicknames they hurled at them.

"Hey, Sweet Tots," Nelson would yell across the street, Coors can in hand and a cooler beside his porch swing. "Where's Milk Duds, your little boyfriend?" It didn't matter whether Donovan feigned indifference or stomped into the house, the reaction was the same. Nelson's redneck friends would howl with laughter, slurp down more beer, and whack their buddy on the back.

"Todd ought to be ashamed of himself for ever acting the way he did," Gwen huffed, hands flanking her hips. "Especially after what Bradley did for Jenna."

"I hear that. When that little Nelson girl chased the soccer ball into the street, I hate to think what would've happened if Bradley hadn't just got home. He threw his briefcase to the ground and snatched Jenna out of the way of an oncoming tractor trailer. You should have heard those brakes squeal as it tried to stop." Donovan shivered at the memory. "Hillary, Todd's wife, she dashed out of the house, but only made it midyard by the time Bradley carried the child to her. Jenna didn't have a scratch on her, but Bradley ripped his pants and skinned his knee pretty bad when he landed on the pavement. Hillary was a crying hysterical mess, hugging Bradley and showering him with thanks. My Bradley's a real hero."

"That story gets me every time I hear it." Gwen sighed and placed her hand over her heart. "Bradley risked his life to save that little girl, even though her dad was such an ass."

Donovan chopped the salad greens, not wanting to verbalize exactly how relieved he was when the hazing stopped.

"You know, Nelson hasn't bothered us one time since that day. He actually walked over here when he got home that afternoon and thanked Bradley for saving Jenna. He sounded sincere, and shook hands with us without wiping his paws on his pants afterward." Donovan grinned at Gwen. "He even invited us over for a beer, which we politely declined. I knew Todd's change of attitude was completely due to gratitude. Even if he never accepts our lifestyle, maybe he can come to understand that we're just ordinary people trying to live our lives."

Now when the Nelson's entertained, they opted to wave politely to the men across the street instead of shouting crude remarks.

The phone rang after Gwen left, just as Donovan placed the ice bucket on the table. "Hello."

"Hi, Donovan. How're you doing?" It was Bradley's mother.

"I'm fine, Mrs. Slaton." They'd always been cordial to each other, even during their initial meeting when it was obvious Bradley's family didn't care for him. Approval or not, they showed good manners to each other. Through the years, Bradley's parents had softened a bit as they became used to the situation. "How are things in Chicago?"

"We're doing fine, thanks for asking. I'm just calling to wish you and Bradley a happy anniversary." Donovan didn't know how to respond, since this was the first time in six years the Slaton's had acknowledged their civil union. Their original stance, as he heard it through the grapevine, was that since the marriage wasn't legally recognized in most states, they didn't intend to recognize it either. After a short silence, Mrs. Slaton cleared her throat. "This *is* the right day, isn't it?"

"Yes, Ma'am. Thank you." Donovan's shock quickly turned to gratitude. "It means a lot to me to hear from you today." They made small talk for a few minutes until Bradley walked through the door, on time as usual.

"Hi," Donovan said, covering the receiver as they exchanged a quick smooch. "Telephone for you." He handed him the phone, not wanting to spoil the surprise of the conversation that awaited him. Seeing Bradley's face light up as he spoke to his mother was an extra gift.

Donovan brought a meal to the dining room that would make Martha Stewart jealous. He lit the candle in the centerpiece he'd bought that afternoon at the cute little flower shop down the street. Yes, this was certainly a special anniversary.

Darci needed some cheering up after she went over the books. April was the first month since she'd opened Petal Pushers that they'd spent so much more than they brought in. Business was still steady, word of her floral talent and personal touches spreading with each order she filled. The problem was the truckloads of slips she bought, since this was the season to plant annuals and perennials after the last frost. That usually happened by the fifteenth, except this year the last frost didn't occurred until the twenty-eighth, which set her projected sales margin back by two weeks.

She fidgeted with her red pencil, the one she used to write negative balances in the ledger, and reminded herself that business was doing exceptionally well for only having been open four short months. "Damn it," she sputtered, startled when the pencil broke in two.

The splintered pieces clanged into the trash can under the counter. Unable to stand another moment working on the ledger, she turned her attention to the parakeet. "Well, Daisy," she said as the bird stepped onto her finger and waddled up to sit on her shoulder, "if the weather doesn't warm up pretty soon, I guess we can market a line of birdseed to bring in some extra bucks."

Petal Pushers' Plant of the Month for March is|

Daffodil
Narcissus hybrids
Perennial Bulb

Common name: Easter flower, Narcissus, and Jonquil.

Brief description: Daffodils vary in height from six inches to two feet. They come in yellow, orange, white, or a combination of those colors, in single and double varieties. Most are scented. This plant is very popular and easy to grow, and can be seen blooming all over the place around Easter. Hoyt Simms' mom, Genevieve, has more varieties blooming in her yard than I've ever seen in one location, so you might want to drive by her home on West Elm Street and take a look.

Symbolism: chivalry, unrequited love, respect, and friendship. It's used as an icon for cancer research.

Trivia: A very old flower first mentioned around 300 BC, the daffodil originated in the area of the

Mediterranean Sea. popular in literature, mentioned in works by William Wordsworth, Tennessee Williams, and e. e. cummings.

Growing instructions: Full sun is best, but these bulbs also do well in dappled shade. Plant these in fall, about twice as deep as the height of the bulbs, six to nine inches apart. If you're going for a naturalized look, toss a handful in the air and plant where they land. These multiply pretty fast, so you can divide the clumps after a few years.

Uses: Scatter daffodils around your yard, under trees and along borders for a sunny burst of color in the spring. They can be grown in containers and make excellent cut flowers.

Tools & Tips: April is a good time to start gardening. You can buy fancy plant markers if you really want, so you can tell your petunias from your squash, but I have a cheaper alternative that works just as well. (Just ask my cousin Charlotte the next time you're in the shop, and she'll be quick to tell you about my frugal ways.) I use a Sharpie marker to label Popsicle sticks with the names of the seeds or slips I plant, and stick them in the ground right beside them. Not fancy but it works, and they'll blend into the background when your garden grows.

Chapter Five

May

*In the dooryard fronting an old farm-house near
the white-wash'd palings,
Stands the lilac-bush tall-growing with
heart-shaped leaves of rich green,
with many a pointed blossom rising delicate,
with the perfume strong I love,
With every leaf a miracle - and from this bush in
the dooryard,
With delicate-color'd blossoms and
heart-shaped leaves of rich green,
A sprig with its flower I break.*
~ Walt Whitman

Charlotte's sigh drew Darci's attention away from
her paperwork. "Something wrong?" Her normally
boisterous cousin wore a forlorn expression, her
eyes fixed on a cup of raspberry tea at the other
end of the counter. She'd been drinking that stuff
by the gallon lately, with plenty of honey to cover

the bitter taste she said reminded her of chicory. Darci thought hormones must be messing with her taste buds, since the tea tasted fine to her by itself.

Darci's jaw dropped open when Charlotte burst into tears, something as far removed from her personality as Vin Diesel dancing Swan Lake in a pink tutu. "What's the matter," she asked, passing her a box of Kleenex.

"Oh my God, Darce. What the hell have I done? I don't think Jimbo and me are ready to be parents." Charlotte blew her nose, threw the saturated Kleenex in the trashcan under the desk, then plucked two more from the box.

"Um, I hate to break it to you, but it's sort of too late to back out now, Miss Preggers." Darci patted her on the back, trying to get her to settle down. She hoped the baby was alright. Charlotte was the closest thing she'd ever have to a sister, and they'd been as thick as thieves growing up. She hated seeing her so upset. "Just calm down and tell me what's on your mind that's got you so worked up."

"I don't think I know what I'm doing. Maybe we're just not responsible enough to take care of a baby yet." Charlotte wiped away the tears streaming down her cheeks as if they were flies buzzing around her head. "Remember that gold-fish I won at the county fair when we were like fourteen? I named her Bubbles?"

"Hey, yeah. I do remember that now." Darci smiled at the memory from their childhood. "You kept it in a glass beer mug by your bed. Your mom's cat got to her one day when we were at school, right?"

"No. That's just the story I made up because I felt so bad," she sniffled, then buried her head in her hands, sobbing even harder. "I forgot to feed the fish and she croaked. I saw her when I woke up one morning, floating belly up in her glass beside an unopened box of fish flakes." She let out a Lucille Ball style wail. Darci could barely understand her through the tears. "Oh my God, I'm so stupid I couldn't even take care of a damn goldfish. I killed Bubbles!"

"Oh. My. Goodness." There were very few times when Darci found herself speechless. Hugging her pregnant cousin as she mourned the death of a fish who died twenty years ago seemed to be one of those times. She opened and closed her mouth until she thought of something to say. "It was just a fish. It's okay."

"Yeah, but how much different is a fish from that egg experiment thing they make kids do in Home Ec? The one where they pretend it's a baby and they get an 'F' if the shell gets cracked or some smartass eats it." Just when Darci thought Charlotte was about to settle down, the floodgates opened again and out came another Lucy groan. "When Bubbles starved to death, I might as well have eaten my baby." She laid her head on the counter and bawled.

"Charlotte, honey, you're gonna have to calm down." Afraid Charlotte was about to make herself sick, Darci decided to use a firmer tone of voice. "Get a grip. What you're feeling are normal pre-baby jitters. Take a few deep breaths and let it pass."

Charlotte lifted her head and mopped her tears with a soggy tissue. "You think so?" The crying slowed to ragged sniffles, her lip quivering slower and slower as she struggled to get a hold of herself. "This is normal?"

"Pretty much." The dead goldfish part was kind of bizarre, but Darci wasn't going to mention that just now. She scooted her chair beside Charlotte's and sat down. "Most of us have some kind of meltdown before the baby comes, so don't worry about it. I woke up one morning when I was seven months pregnant with Paxton and got hysterical. The only thing that kept running through my mind was 'what if I can't tell when he's hungry'. I couldn't for the life of me figure out how I would know when the kid wanted to eat. How stupid was that?" Darci laughed, but Charlotte's eyes grew bigger.

"So, how *did* you know when to feed Paxton? I hadn't thought of that yet."

"Oh, hell no. I'm not giving you something else to worry about. I'm trying to show you how ridiculous the idea was. The kid will scream his freakin' head off when he gets hungry. Unless you've got industrial strength earplugs, no way are you and Jimbo going to sleep through it."

"What if the baby gets that thing, that colic I read about in my *Mommy 2 B* book? I read a bunch of stuff about it, but I still don't really understand what the hell I'm supposed to do if the kid starts that non-stop screaming."

"If the baby gets colic, you can always bring him or her into the shop. We can set up the play-pen over there by the porthole and let our resi-dent ghost take care of it. If she can bring plants back from the dead, she should be able to cure a little tummy ache. Just think of all the money you can save on medical bills."

Charlotte glared at her, apparently unamused by Darci's attempt to lighten the mood.

An icy warning settled on the back of her neck, the chill lingering even as Darci attempted to warm her nape with the palm of her hand. She figured she'd better change the subject and wipe the grin off her face before Charlotte knocked it off, or the ghost gave her a bad case of frostbite. "Okay, so what did the article say you should do?"

"Put the car seat on a washing machine set to the spin cycle, but that just sounded kind of dumb." Charlotte must have felt a little better be-cause her eyes twinkled. "Jimbo and me did something else on our washing machine when we were trying to conceive the kid, but that's a whole other story."

The second Saturday in May meant Prom time for local high school students. With kids coming in to order corsages and boutonnieres for weeks preceding the dance, Petal Pushers stayed busy. After some urging from his buddy Hoyt, the chairman of the decorating committee hired Darci to make all the swags, centerpieces, and balloons, plus a special display beside which the photographer would snap pictures of teenage couples decked out in their formal attire and goofy grins.

Darci was exhausted, but gleefully so. Business boomed right along, with a steady stream of customers flowing through to buy vegetable slips and annuals from the greenhouse to plant in their gardens and flower beds. Darci didn't mind the extra work at all, since she and Hoyt were perfectly capable of handling it themselves. Charlotte was just seven weeks away from her due date, so Darci hated to ask her to do anything more strenuous than answering the phone. Charlotte insisted she loved her job and enjoyed getting out of the house while she was still able to, but it was obvious she'd hit the point in her pregnancy where comfort pretty much eluded her.

On Prom morning, Charlotte dealt with excited teenagers who came in to pick up corsages to bedeck their gowns and rental tuxedos. Darci took a vanload of decorations to the high school gymnasium, Hoyt having hauled the balloons over by himself beforehand. A swarm of eager kids from the decorating committee helped unload everything, then did a nice job of setting things up.

Darci insisted on working on the photographer's backdrop herself, to make sure the potted elephant ear and birds of paradise conveyed the tropical feel the senior class picked for their theme. A wave of nostalgia hit Darci before she left; she wished she and Wade could sneak in and crash the fun. The idea got funnier the more she thought about it, since it was something Charlotte might very well try to pull off-if she'd been hitting the tequila instead of being seven months pregnant. Oh well, they'd just have to be satisfied to live vicariously through Hoyt this time, who she and Charlotte would grill for Prom details come Monday.

When she arrived back at the shop that afternoon, she held the door open for a cute teenage girl. She recognized her since she'd been in the shop a few times before, to hang fresh SADD posters in the front window, but today she carried a red carnation in a small clear-plastic box. Darci stifled a sigh and imagined the memories the girl would make tonight after she pinned the boutonniere to her boyfriend's lapel. "Have fun at the Prom."

"Great news," Charlotte announced as soon as Darci walked behind the counter. "I do believe I've finally found the person to hire as a babysitter, one of Hoyt's friends. You just passed her on your way in."

Ashley Rosales had dreamed of Prom night ever since she was in fourth grade and watched her older cousin Gloria transform herself from a soccer-playing tomboy into a gown-wearing princess. Tonight, it was Ashley's turn to be Cinderella.

She wanted to roll the windows down on her

Mustang, to breathe the fresh air on this beautiful spring day. Unfortunately, she couldn't risk messing up her hair-do. Good thing the light wind hadn't tousled it when she made her pit stop at Petal Pushers. Two hours of her life had gone into sitting in the Hair Dare Your 'Do Salon, having her hair washed, conditioned, blow-dried, set on hot rollers, then arranged in place with bobby pins after a few tresses were wrapped around the barrel of a curling iron. The vent would be as close as she was going to come to feeling a fresh breeze in the car. Ashley cranked up her Nickelback CD and daydreamed about the Prom on her way home, picturing herself as a fairytale princess. Her heart raced when she thought of Jordan Cooley, her very own Prince Charming.

Ashley and Jordan had been dating for about three months now. She'd had boyfriends before, but none who made her feel as special as Jordan did. She could tell by his sincere words and actions that he loved her, that he didn't just feel sorry for her like some of the other kids.

"They're coming up the driveway, Ash," her mom called up the stairs later that evening. "Are you ready, or do you want me to stall them for a few minutes?"

"Be right down," Ashley called back, happiness and excitement ringing in her voice. She smiled at her reflection in the full-length mirror that hung on the back of her bedroom door. The lavender gown brought out her green eyes, and the matching pumps were actually comfortable. All the practice she'd put into walking would come in handy tonight; she was confident she wouldn't limp or fall on her face. She paused in front of her dresser for a last minute touch-up, then lifted the chestnut waves that fell over her right shoulder to apply a little more concealer to the scar on the side of her neck. Her mother said it wasn't noticeable, but Ashley still felt self-conscious about it. She fluffed her hair with her fingers-no way she'd run a brush through these hairspray-shellacked ringlets and risk dragging out the curls-dabbed on a touch more lip gloss, and blotted her kisser on a Kleenex before she headed downstairs.

She'd never seen the bunch so dressed up before. They looked like movie stars ready to stroll down the red carpet. Ashley's dad snapped a ton of pictures as she and Jordan stood flanked by the other two couples, Ashley's best friend Amber and Hoyt to their left, and Kirsten and Eddie to their right. I'm so lucky to have made it to this night, Ashley thought, sandwiched between her friends, straining not to blink at the flash.

A black stretch limo carried the three couples to a posh restaurant in downtown Henderson. Fear of dribbling food on her gown didn't dull Ashley's appetite as she savored each and every bite. While Amber nibbled a Caesar salad and drank water because it wouldn't stain her ebony cocktail dress, Ashley chowed down on pineapple-grilled chicken and mushroom risotto, which she washed down with a glass of sweet tea. All the guys opted for steak and potatoes, a meal for the macho as Hoyt called it. When the dessert cart rolled around, Amber shot an envious glance towards Ashley's Bananas Foster.

"Ugh, this mess-proof macaroon just doesn't measure up to *that*. Guess it's the price I have to pay for not ruining the dress I worked all winter to pay for." Amber bit off a piece of her somewhat dry coconut cookie without much enthusiasm. "Does that taste as good as it smells?"

"Here, open up." With the linen napkin held under her loaded spoon, being oh so careful not to dribble the sauce, Ashley popped a bite into Amber's mouth. Her rolling eyes and moan of gratitude made Ashley laugh. "No thanks necessary. That's what BFFs are for."

A foot nudged her under the table, drawing her attention across the elegant centerpiece toward Jordan. "Hey, why does she get all the attention?" The tea lights made his hazel eyes glow as he winked at her.

"Okay, I guess I can spare a bite for you, since you *are* paying for my meal . . . and you *do* look smokin' hot in that tux." Ashley fed Jordan a bite of her dessert, tempted to kiss the sugary speck that lingered on his bottom lip. She opted to wipe it with her napkin instead, since they were in a public place and the other diners weren't likely to appreciate seeing her stick her tongue down his throat.

Hoyt, handsome as ever with Amber on his tuxedo clad arm, led the way to the parking lot. "Next stop, the Prom." With a theatrical flourish, he held open the car door for the young ladies, then gave a comical curtsy to his buds before climbing in behind the girls.

Ashley was stunned by the magical atmosphere when they walked in. Flowers and twinkle lights transformed the school gym into a one-night paradise for the seniors and their dates. Tropical potpourri lent an exotic fragrance to complete the night's theme. (The principal vetoed the decorating committee's request for candles, since Tommy Hinkerman used one at the Homecoming dance to set the streamers on fire.) One by one, the three couples took turns posing for the photographer in front of a gorgeous backdrop, complete with exotic flowers Hoyt said were bird of paradise plants.

Seated at their table, the girls discussed everyone's outfits while their dates talked about Eddie's new classic convertible, an early graduation present from his grandpa. When the Black Eyed Peas song "Imma Be" came through the speakers, will.i.am and Fergie's voices drew them to the dance floor.

Ashley didn't care how graceful she looked. During all those months of relearning how to walk, this Prom was the proverbial carrot on a stick she'd held out in front of herself. She learned to walk without a cane, thanks in large part to all those hours spent with Bella Rose, her Arabian mare, with Cyril Maldonado at her other side coaxing her to take so many additional steps before leaning on her horse for support. She could almost feel her friend and mentor smiling down at her, something that gave her a combination of pride, comfort, and the sting of sentimental tears in the corner of her eye. She blinked them away. Right now she just wanted to move to the music, letting the beat guide her feet as she looked into Jordan's eyes, his hands resting on the small of her back during the slow songs.

Punch filled Ashely's bladder, which prompted her and the other two girls to visit the ladies room. On the way back to the gym after they'd relieved themselves and reapplied varying shades of pink lipstick, she passed one of the posters she'd designed hanging on the bulletin board near the office. The local chapter of Students Against Drunk Drivers, SADD for short, had posted over a hundred such fliers around the county.

She touched the scar on her right arm between her elbow and wrist, reminded once again of how lucky she was to be there, dancing the night away with her friends. The poster sent her thoughts drifting back to a less than happy time in her life.

On a beautiful spring afternoon two years before, Ashley left Amber's house on her bicycle to make it home in time for supper. A blue sedan filled with college kids on their way to a ballgame ran a stoplight and plowed into Ashley's side as she pedaled across the street. The bumper broke her left femur when it rammed her leg; the splintered bone poked through her skin between her knee and denim shorts. Thrown through the air from the impact, she landed on her right side, her head and arm hitting the asphalt with a sickening crunch she still heard in her nightmares. The doctors told her later-much later, after two surgeries when she finally regained consciousness-that it was a miracle she'd been thrown, rather than dragged under the wheels like her mangled Schwinn. No way could she have survived that.

Pins held her leg bone together, and an orthopedic surgeon worked hard to insure her arm healed correctly aligned. Broken bones held a special kind of pain all their own-a sort of intense throbbing, like a migraine in her marrow-something she found difficult to explain when her parents asked how she felt. Her neck made the injuries in her arm and leg seem like mild irritations.

Unconscious for days after the accident due to a serious concussion, she awoke to find her head stuck in a contraption that looked like something out of a bad science fiction movie. Called a halo, the metal frame sat on her shoulders and extended above her head; the top of the thing actually screwed into her skull to keep the vertebrae in her neck still while they healed. At least she wasn't paralyzed.

Her recovery was a long, slow process, during which she coped with pain no teenager should have to go through. Medication helped during the initial weeks, but, not wanting her to become addicted to the strong narcotics, they cut the dosage back as soon as they were able. When the halo and her casts came off, the real hell of her recovery started. Rehab. Her mother couldn't tolerate staying in the room, unable to endure her daughter's screams as atrophied muscles worked to regain use of her arm, leg, and neck. Her father gritted his teeth alongside Ashley, and tears spilled over his cheeks on more than one occasion.

Physical therapy started the same week nineteen-year-old Josh Tabor was convicted of hit and run, drunk driving, possession of alcohol by a minor, and a few other charges Ashley couldn't recall. She memorized the photo of him that appeared on the front page of the county paper and pictured his face each agonizing time she did her exercises, while her therapist coached her to move just a little more each day through searing pain. Hating Tabor more than she'd ever hated any living being, she spent sleepless pain-wracked nights wishing he'd been sentenced to be strapped to a railroad track, like in the old silent movies, and then have a locomotive rip him in half. Justice would be his feeling the agony she suffered, not having him sit in jail munching on bologna sandwiches beside the TV all day, while she was in too much pain to swallow hospital gruel.

One day the nurse put a letter on Ashley's dinner tray, beside the untouched mystery meat and a glob of mashed potatoes the consistency of wallpaper paste. Ashley flicked off the television with the remote control built into the side of the hospital bed, then picked up the envelope, expecting it to be another get well card to add to the growing collection set up on the table under the wall-mounted TV.

She started the arduous process of opening the envelope, refusing to call the nurse in to help her. It was bad enough that the medical staff still had to help her in and out of the bathroom. She'd only been in physical therapy one week so her right arm hung practically useless, just mobile enough to get in her way. While it was in the cast, Ashley had gotten pretty dexterous with her other hand. She held the letter still with the three fingers on the pinky side of her left hand as her index finger and thumb worked a hole under the flap until it opened, then she unfolded the stationary within.

She couldn't believe her eyes as she read the closing. With the letter crumpled into a lopsided paper cannonball, she hurled it across the room where it landed in a corner, soon to be joined by the wadded up envelope. How dare that bastard write a letter to compensate for the fact he'd nearly killed her. No way was she going to read it. Screw him!

She stared at the stark white wall across from her bed until her seething rage subsided. Her thoughts turned to curiosity. What could Tabor possibly have to say? She glanced at the letter on the floor and her hackles rose all over again. With her leg fresh out of the cast, she couldn't even get out of bed to pick the damn thing up if she wanted to.

An orderly popped in later to take her lunch tray, so Ashley asked him to hand her the letter. Alone in her room, she smoothed the paper out and read it:

Dear Ashley Rosales,

I'm writing to tell you how very sorry I am for what happened· I know these are only words and won't do anything to make your injuries hurt less, but it's important for me to apologize for what I did· I was a damn idiot· Most of the accident is a blur in my memory, except for the vision burned into my mind of you lying in a twisted heap at the side of the road· That image wakes me up screaming in my cell at night·

I know you probably hate me, and you have every right to feel that way· It would be great if you could find it in your heart to forgive me one day, though I'm not asking you to· I hope you get better soon, and have a full recovery and a happy life· Please know how horrible I feel and that I'm very, very sorry·

Sincerely,
Josh Tabor

Her hatred melted into indifference, but not

pity and not quite forgiveness. He made a conscious choice to drink and drive, a decision she paid for. The apology validated her feelings somehow, and let her move past the hate and get on with her recovery, mentally as well as physically.

"Come on, silly." Amber grabbed her elbow and pulled her back toward the gym. "This night's not gonna last forever, you know."

Ashley had the time of her life. She savored every moment of happiness, knowing how easily life could slip away without a moment's notice.

"Phone, Darce," Charlotte bellowed loudly enough to be heard in the work room where Darci was busy putting the finishing touches on the last order of Memorial Day arrangements, these made from artificial flowers that would stay pretty longer in the cemetery, honoring loved ones who've passed on. "It's Wade."

"Hello." Darci heard Charlotte hang up the other receiver in the main room.

"You very busy, Hon?" From the sugary tone of his voice, she could tell she was about to get even busier.

"No worse than usual. Why?"

"Last night Paxton was playing around with my stuff and he didn't put my level back in the tool box," Wade explained. "I promised Teresa Nolan I'd get her new kitchen cabinets finished by sundown. She's having a fancy brunch thing tomorrow morning, so she'll get her panties all in a bunch if everything isn't perfect." He'd whispered the last sentence into his cell phone.

"Well, we wouldn't want that."

"If you could swing by the house and then bring it to me, I sure would appreciate it. It's the new level with the laser on it, and I think he left it in the laundry room. He was playing alien invasion and the washing machine was supposed to be the White House."

"No problem." Darci grabbed a notepad to jot down the address. "Be there in about half an hour. Love you. Bye." Yep, lucky for Wade she liked running her hands through his thick blonde hair, and the way his mustache tickled when he gave her a goodbye kiss each morning. Otherwise, she might not be so eager to drop everything for him. She really didn't mind too much, since Charlotte could run the place while she was out.

Surely enough, Wade's fancy new level was on top of the washing machine beside a toy space ship. She smiled and imagined Paxton, his sweet little face twisted in mock seriousness as he defended the planet from a bunch of little green Martians.

Mrs. Nolan answered the doorbell when Darci found the house. "Hi, I'm Wade's wife. He wanted me to drop this thing off for him," she explained, holding up the tool.

"Come on in. He's in the kitchen, just through those doors. You've got to see the beautiful cherry cabinets he made for me. Oh, the girls from the book club will be so jealous when they see them tomorrow."

"I'm glad you're happy with the cabinets. I know the sketches he showed me were to die for." Darci's heart swelled with pride to see how satisfied Mrs. Nolan was with Wade's work. "Your garden is absolutely spectacular, by the way. Do you tend it yourself or do you have a gardener?"

"Thank you, dear. No, I enjoy my flowers too much to let anybody else have all the fun. Except for my son, of course. He comes over every Sunday afternoon and helps with the hard jobs and weed pullin' where it's snaky. Can I offer you a cup of coffee?"

"Oh, no thank you. I need to be getting back to the shop. I'll just run this to Wade and be on my way," she said, remembering the level she held in her hands. "It was nice to meet you."

Darci walked to the kitchen through the living room, past a display of family photographs arranged on the sofa table. Nice looking relatives. One vaguely familiar man with sandy brown hair filled quite a few picture frames, some with him on horseback and one of him hugging an older gentleman she assumed to be his father, though she didn't see any family resemblance.

When Darci headed back to her car, she couldn't help but stop to take one more look at the gorgeous border around the Nolan's yard. Tinged with just a hint of red, leaves the size of garbage can lids blended beautifully with the lilacs growing on one side and the sweet peas that scrolled up the fence to the right. That plant

would be the perfect thing to fill in a corner behind the greenhouse. She stopped herself from
going back to ask the lady of the house what it
was called, since she figured it wouldn't exactly
make her look like a knowledgeable florist. No,
she would look it up in one of her gardening volumes back at the shop.

**Petal Pushers' Plant of the Month for May
is**

**Bird of Paradise
Strelitzia reginae
Perennial**

Common name: Crane Flowers.

Brief description: A native to South Africa, this unusual blossom looks like a bird in flight or a bird's head and beak, depending on how you look at it. The blooms are usually yellow, blue, and orange. The plant can reach four feet in height, with foliage that resembles a banana leaf.

Symbolism: freedom and faithfulness.

Trivia: These beautiful plants are actually poisonous, so please keep them away from children and pets.

Growing instructions: This plant is more of a challenge, but well worth it. They need moderate to bright sunlight, and heavy waterings to keep the soil moist. If grown outdoors, it must be brought inside when the temperature falls below fifty degrees. Use a quality peat-based potting soil and fertilize regularly. Bird of Paradise plants

95

don't usually flower until they're about five years old.

Uses: Birds of Paradise are unforgettable in a landscape, make an extraordinary houseplant, and are beautiful in flower arrangements.

Tools & Tips: We just got a shipment of Garden Journals in at Petal Pushers, just in time for Mother's Day. These handy little books let you keep track of what you plant where each year, keep notes about everything garden related, sketch out new ideas, and make lists of plants and supplies you need to pick up on your next trip to town. Garden journals make excellent gifts, or a nice treat for yourself.

Vera Thompkins ordered another Bird of Paradise plant last week. She's Webster County's expert on this plant, since she has two others at home she's kept alive since her daughter gave them to her as a birthday gift nine years ago. Vera's the one to ask if you need advice on your Bird of Paradise. She works over at Golden Days Retirement Home and loves to talk plants during her afternoon coffee break.

Chapter Six

June

The old tree is shook
White blossoms slowly float down
Dancers in the wind
~ Alexandra Kim

Sparrows in the trees overhead chirped as dappled sunlight illuminated the grass underfoot. With Hoyt's help, Darci set plants around, finding the perfect place for each in the border that encircled Golden Days Retirement Home. The mild weather, which hadn't climbed above the breezy lower eighties, made it a joy to come to work.

Darci stood back and scrutinized the layout before planting any slips in the soil. The red impatiens and monkey grass, which would sport small purple florets later in the season, were the perfect choices for the border. Their bright blooms over the dark green foliage should be visible even to people with failing vision.

Along with the beds edging the retirement home, they set red Knock Out roses around benches placed on either side of the yard. People could sit and enjoy their perfume just out of reach of the thorns. A sidewalk running from the front door to the street divided the lawn down the middle. Another thing on Darci's To-Do list was to line either side of the walkway with perennial herbs. Fresh thyme, sage, oregano, and lavender would bloom in various shades of purple, white, and pink throughout the season and smell heavenly as residents strolled past them. They'd easily bounce back if stepped on, plus the cook could snip pieces off whenever she liked for tasty additions to fresh soups and casseroles.

The fresh summer air and the scent of rich dirt filled Darci's lungs and made her feel like she was in her own little corner of gardener's heaven. She grabbed her trowel and went to work planting the impatiens and monkey grass while Hoyt tilled around the edge of the sidewalk. She almost felt sorry for Charlotte, stuck in the shop on such a beautiful day.

On her knees in the middle of the border, Darci had the strangest feeling someone was watching her. She just couldn't shake the sensation. Why anyone would take an interest in a chubby florist, she had no idea, but hoped the new highlights Donovan finally talked her into last week weren't to blame. Pretending to stretch, she stood up and turned around to face the yard behind her. No one glanced her way.

As she reached for another clump of monkey

grass, an elderly woman caught her eye. Perched on a lawn chair under a tulip poplar some distance away, she gazed in Darci's general direction from under cover of the shade tree. The lady noticed that she'd been spotted and immediately feigned interest in the open magazine on her lap. Darci paused a minute, planning to wave if she looked back up, though she never did. Must be either shy or ornery, Darci decided, then shrugged and went back to work.

With the plants set, she spread pine mulch around them and filled in the border. The lady in the shade was watching her again. Darci approached her, intent on making a little small talk before she started on the herbs. "Hi," she said, still about five yards away. "Isn't this a nice day we're having?"

Startled, the woman jumped up, grabbed her cane, and ambled toward the rest home as quickly as her limp allowed. Her gaze on the ground ahead of her, she offered a timid wave when she hurried past. The magazine she'd been reading fell to the ground in her haste to get away.

Darci picked it up. "Excuse me, Ma'am. I think this is yours. Ma'am?" The woman ignored her, but limped faster.

"Here, I'll take it to her." Another resident who'd been sitting on one of the benches came up to Darci and took the magazine. "And don't take it personally. That was Mrs. Guthrie and she don't talk to anybody."

"Thanks. I was afraid I forgot to wear my deodorant this morning," Darci said, smiling at the spunky older lady who stood in front of her wearing rolled up jeans, sandals, and a big straw hat.

"No sweetie, you smell fine." She grinned back, her eyes sparkling through the shadow of her hat. "Mabel moved in here, oh, about a year ago, I think. Our kids were in the same class in elementary school, quite a while back. She used to be outgoing and sociable, but all that changed after the stroke."

"It looked like she was moving pretty fast, to me."

"She manages pretty well with the cane. She could be a whole lot better, but she flat out refuses to do the rehab exercises the doctor gave her. Her left side is partially paralyzed, so that arm and leg don't work so good, and you can see it on that side of her face. The heifer is so vain, she won't talk because her speech is a little fuddled. Her daughter told me she can understand her just fine, but her sentences are kind of broken and some of the words come out slurred."

"Oh, that's too bad." Darci's big heart felt heavy, saddened to hear that Mrs. Guthrie had such a hard time of it. The woman in the straw hat noticed her biting her lip and fidgeting with her belt loops, so Darci shoved her hands in her pockets to keep them still.

"You're doing a fine job on that flower bed. And I'm Bernice, by the way." She adjusted her hat as Darci introduced herself, then the two walked toward the newly planted border. "Always did love those everyday bloomers."

"That's what my mom calls impatiens too."

"Well, I guess I'd better let you get back at it, and I'll see that Mabel gets her copy of *Better Homes and Gardens*." Bernice bounded up the stairs like a teenager. "Nice to meet you."

"Nice meeting you, too. You'll have to let me know what you think of the rest of the landscaping, after we get finished with it." Darci liked Bernice, who reminded her a little of her great-Aunt Becky.

Puddles of rain poured from the sky before they finished laying weed cloth on either side of the walk. No use trying to fight a thunderstorm. Darci and Hoyt hurried to load their stuff back into the van, hoping the lightning wouldn't strike the gardening tools they carried.

The warm weather dried the ground out enough for them to get back to work the next morning. Darci arranged the Knock Out rosebushes around the benches on opposite sides of the lawn. Hoyt planted them, then piled mulch around each when he finished.

Next, Darci positioned herbs on top of the black weed cloth, making sure to space them correctly. The spiky lavender leaves already smelled heavenly, and she couldn't wait until they bloomed. Alternating them with the thyme, sage, and oregano for an informal feel, she grabbed her trowel and got busy tucking them into the ground. This was her favorite part of a job like this, getting her hands in the dirt, knowing these plants would look and smell great for a long time to come. Unlike the impatiens, these herbs were perennials that should come back hardier year

101

after year.

Mabel Guthrie sat under the tulip poplar again. Not wanting to make her feel uncomfortable, Darci tried not to pay any attention.

On her knees mulching the herbs, she heard feet shuffle over the sidewalk in her direction. Her hand shaded her eyes from the glare of the sun as she peeped up and was pleasantly surprised to see Mabel in front of her, leaning heavily on her cane.

"Hi there." She started to comment on the weather, but didn't want to say anything that would put the elderly woman in a position of having to speak.

The right side of Mabel's mouth tried to curl upward while the left side of her face hung flaccid. She took a deep breath, nodded her head toward the plants, and with a laborious effort to shape her lips correctly, said, "Pretty."

"Thank you, Mrs. Guthrie. I'm glad you like it. They should fill in in a week or so, then they'll really smell nice when you walk by, especially if there's a breeze." Darci kept on placing mulch, making it unnecessary for Mabel to reply. She looked up when Mabel cleared her throat.

Mrs. Guthrie pointed her gaze toward the magazine sticking out of her tote bag. Darci figured she used it to carry things, since her left arm hung limp at her side and the cane barred her from holding anything in her right hand. After another deep breath, she said, "Thanks," in reference to Darci's attempt to return it to her the day before.

"No problem. I get that magazine myself and wouldn't want you to lose it. Great articles this month, and a tasty recipe for hummingbird cake, though it's not quite as good as my Grandma Odette's version."

Darci stood up after she pinched off a generous sprig of the lavender she'd been fidgeting with. "I just love how this stuff smells." She held it up to Mabel, who closed her eyes and sniffed the intoxicating fragrance.

"Here you go, Mrs. Guthrie." Darci tucked the lavender sprig into the tote bag. "So you can enjoy it later."

Gratitude glistened in her eyes. She attempted to say her name, which Darci took to mean she wished to be addressed more informally. It came out sounding more like 'Mail' than 'Mabel', which caused her to glare at her shoes in humiliation.

Darci was glad Bernice had filled her in. "Nice to meet you, Mabel." The older lady lifted her eyes to meet Darci's, obviously relieved to be understood. "I'm Darci."

Mabel lifted two fingers from her cane in a wave, then turned and headed back inside.

Custodians at Golden Days Retirement home watered the landscape regularly, but Petal Pushers came by every other week to maintain the plants. It didn't take long since the weed cloth prevented most problems, though some pesky grasses put down roots in the mulch on top of it. When Darci swung by, she'd pull up any stray weeds, deadhead the climbing roses that grew on the backyard trellis, and pinch back some of the herbs to make them grow in bushier. She looked forward to spending time there, stretching a thirty-minute job out for an hour in the tranquil garden, happy to shoot the breeze with the friendly residents.

Paxton enjoyed spending summer days at the shop with his mother. He had water gun fights with Hoyt out back, tried unsuccessfully to teach Daisy how to say "Paxton Rules", and carried things for Charlotte, who now waddled around like a constipated duck. Pride showed in the way he carried himself when he helped his mom; standing tall, his shoulders squared, he would glance around to see if anyone noticed how grown up he thought he was. Darci was so proud of him, she didn't even mind when he made the occasional mistake.

One such blunder was Paxton's overzealous tendency with the watering can, which he wielded until muddy streams flowed over the sides of the containers. Fortunately, most of the greenhouse slips recovered on their own. They'd just skip watering them for a few days until the humidity steered the moisture level in their potting soil back to where it should be. Some plants, however, just couldn't handle a flood.

After Wade picked Paxton up for a trip to town for fishing bait one afternoon, Hoyt brought a flat of chamomile to Darci's attention. "Um, I think he overdid it a little," he said, tilting the plastic container to drain off the excess water. Being the second day in a row they'd received this treatment, the tiny leaves showed more brown than green.

"Oh boy." Darci winced her sympathy at the soaking plants. "If you could transfer these to a dry tray, we can put 'em inside the shop for a couple days. Maybe that'll help."

Later, Darci moved a small table over by the porthole window, then put the chamomile in the light that filtered in through the trees outside.

For some reason she couldn't explain or understand, she and Charlotte noticed strange occurrences on a regular basis. The temperature climbed up in the eighties, but they still felt cold drafts behind the counter and in front of the porthole. Wade couldn't find any source, and it even happened when the air conditioning wasn't on.

Every few days, Charlotte thought she saw a woman in a long dark dress. On entering the room or looking up from paperwork, she'd catch a glimpse of someone at the porthole or a figure peering into Daisy's cage. During and right after those incidents, Daisy tweeted nonstop, bobbing her head happily as she jumped from perch to perch; she usually only acted that way when someone talked to her, in the hopes of coming out of the cage to play.

The oddest phenomenon, though, had to be the reason Darci set the overwatered chamomile in front of the porthole-shaped window. The spider plant she and Charlotte found in March, which miraculously thrived after being a prickly dried out mess the night before, had been the first of such unprecedented floral healings. When Charlotte found a potted rosebush with black and yellow leaves-something that usually meant stripping leaves off and applying medicated powder-she placed it on the stool in front of the porthole. Rubbing her hands together manically after setting it down, Charlotte had said, "Now we'll wait and see what happens. If those leaves are green tomorrow, we'll know it's either the work of E.T., a stray leprechaun, or some funky little greenhouse fairy."

"And to make sure nobody's punking us," Darci said, leaning over the rosebush, "I'll draw a little blue 'x' on the underside of this leaf, so we'll know for sure if it's the same plant." Charlotte took another bathroom break and Darci hid the Sharpie in a box of Daisy's bird food.

The next morning, all traces of black and yellow on the leaves had inexplicably vanished. When Charlotte got to work, Darci made her sit down before showing her the bush, afraid the excitement might freak her out and send her into premature labor. Darci just about wet her own pants when she saw the healthy plant. She had to sit down and breathe into a paper bag after her shaky hand tipped up a healthy green leaf marked with the blue Sharpie 'x'. Charlotte took it much better, wide eyed, fascinated, and grinning like an idiot.

From then on, puny flora went straight to the stool beside the porthole. If the container was too big, like the cement planter holding a fungus-covered topiary, it went on the floor in front of the window.

Darci checked on the chamomile plants right before closing time. Still brown and droopy.

She retrieved her purse and car keys from the counter, but when she turned back around to leave, she froze in her tracks and gasped. An icy shiver raced down her spine. Whatever she thought she saw disappeared in the time it took to blink her eyes. The temperature, however, remained at least twenty degrees cooler than it had been a moment before. Darci grabbed her stuff and walked backward out of the shop. No way was she turning her back, just in case what she saw was an intruder instead of a hallucination. She locked the door behind her, then ran to her car parked in the side driveway. Her cell phone was out of her purse and ringing Charlotte's house before she pulled the door of her green Volkswagen Beetle closed. She locked the car doors, let up her windows, and turned the key simultaneously.

Comforted slightly by her cousin's "Hello", Darci tried to calm herself down. She didn't want to sound hysterical when she got to the crux of the matter.

"Hey, Charlotte. How's it going?"

"Fine. Boring. You know how it is. I'm just sitting here, fat and swollen, downing Tums to kill this damn heartburn. Having a ball. Whoopee." When the line remained silent for a moment, Charlotte asked, concerned, "What's the matter,

Darce? Something wrong?"

"No, not really . . . . Uh, I think I just saw your disappearing lady. Scared the shit out of me, to tell the truth."

"Aha! So it's not just the loony prego seeing things! I told you so."

"Gee, you don't have to sound so thrilled about it." Some of the tension drained from Darci's shoulders. Charlotte's voice made her feel better, even with the 'I told you so'.

"Sorry, you know me. Just can't help myself." Chips crunched in the background, and Charlotte's mouth sounded full when she continued. "So. What the hell did you see?"

"I turned around and thought I saw a woman in old-timey clothes behind the counter next to Daisy's cage. The bird sounded happy, tweeting a mile a minute. The woman, if that's what it was, reached toward the cage, then I blinked and she was gone. Poof. And I was standing in a cold spot." Darci shivered behind the steering wheel. "Gives me the willies thinking about it."

"Sounds like the same thing I saw," Charlotte muttered through another mouthful. Darci heard her swallow. "So, do you think we're haunted or what?"

"Either that or somebody's playing a joke on us. Though with you about to drop the baby, I don't really think anybody would be that stupid right now." She gripped the wheel with one hand while the other fiddled with the thin wire connecting her earpiece to the cell phone; a Bluetooth was on her want list, but she hadn't sprung for one yet. Darci needed to make sure they'd both seen the same thing, that her imagination wasn't just working overtime. She nibbled her lip before asking the question, unsure which answer she hoped to hear. "Did your woman have on anything else you remember, besides the long dark dress? Hat, jewelry?"

"No hat, for sure. I remember her hair was all piled up on top of her head. Definitely could have used a haircut and some curlers. Hmmm . . ." Charlotte munched something else, deep in thought. "Come to think of it, there was a shiny thing on her blouse, like a pin or something."

Fresh goose pimples rose on Darci's arms despite the warm June temperature. "I saw it, too. A broach worn on her left side. No way we could both be having the exact same hallucination."

"Nope, I wouldn't think so." A belch blasted through the cell.

"Yuck."

"Sorry. These damn chips make me burp. Taste good on the way down, though."

"The Ghost Lady must be causing the drafts, too. Oh crap, now I sound like Hoyt, but Ghost Lady is the only thing I can think of to call her right now. Anyway, Paxton waterlogged the chamomile again, so I had just checked the plants in front of the porthole when all this stuff happened. I turned toward the counter, saw the Ghost Lady or whatever the hell it was, then it was so cold I actually saw my breath."

"Well, I bet the chamomile will be healthy by the time we go in tomorrow morning. At least she's saving you some money." Charlotte grunted through the phone as if exerting a massive effort. "Gotta go pee again, Darce. See you in the morning."

"Bye." Darci unhooked the earpiece and clicked the phone off, talking to herself as she pulled in her driveway. "At least it's a helpful ghost, not some screaming banshee or headless, bloody, icky thing. It could be a lot worse."

It didn't come as a surprise the next morning when each and every chamomile plant stood healthy and thriving.

Petal Pushers' Plants of the Month for June are

Common Herbs
Perennial and Annual

Brief description: I love growing my own herbs, for the way they look, smell, and, oh yes, the way they taste. They're easy to grow, then you can snip them as your kitchen demands. Here's the scoop on some of my favorite herbs.

Basil (*Ocimum basilicum*), an annual, is what I'd choose if I could only grow one. Its fragrant broad green leaves are delicious in my homemade red sauce, in omelets, and a million other recipes. So much better than the dried stuff.

Oregano (*Origanum vulagare*), a perennial, is the best variety for cooking. It has small dark green leaves and its flowers vary between white and light purple. Use fresh chopped oregano in your sauces, soups, and salads, and dry a little of the extra.

Thyme (*Thymus vulgaris*), a perennial, is

a short plant with small green leaves. There's nothing better to jazz up your eggs and omelets, and it gives a wonderful earthy flavor to meats and vegetable dishes.

Sage (Salvia *officinalis*), a shrubby perennial with elongated green leaves, it can grow up to two feet tall and have a three foot spread. I grow a few varieties in my herb patch, for the different scents, foliage, and flavors. I love Pineapple sage (*Salvia elegans*), with its delicious tropical taste and showy red blossoms.

Chives (*Allium schoenoprasm*), a perennial, grows in clumps that produce starry white blooms. Snip the leaves for soups, sandwiches, or whenever you want to add a mild onion/garlic flavor.

Mint (*Mentha x piperita*), a perennial, has a peppermint flavor, dark purple stems, green leaves, and smells like a candy cane.

Spearmint (*Mentha spicata*) has dark green pointed leaves and reminds me of chewing gum when I catch a whiff of it. Mint is a hardy herb that spreads easily, and the scent carries in the wind or when you walk over it. Use mint for brewing your own tea, in jelly, with green peas, and in salads.

Symbolism: Like flowers, herbs have their own language, symbolizing certain qualities:

Basil - Clarity and prosperity
Oregano - Joy and happiness
Thyme - Courage and health
Sage - Wisdom, immortality, and respect
Chives - Eternity
Mint - Virtue

Growing instructions: Most herbs do well in a sunny location with regular waterings. Pinch back the tops just before or right as they bloom to encourage a bushier plant and more growth. Don't pitch the flowers you just pinched, but use them as edible garnish or add them to salads for an elegant touch and a bit of extra flavor.

Uses: Herbs are so versatile, they can be used in an herb garden, mixed in flower beds and borders, and in containers. Or put a few potted plants in your kitchen window, for easy access while you cook. One warning: be careful of where you plant mint, which can take over the garden before you know it.

Tools & Tips: Spent up all your flower budget and forgot to buy mulch? No problem. Grass clippings spread pretty thick will stop weed growth. At first, I was leery of this tip because I

was afraid it would make grass grow in my flowerbeds, but it doesn't, and it really does a great
job of keeping the weeds out. After you mow the
yard, just rake up a pile and use it to mulch
around your vegetable garden or other plants. I
also use it around flowers in containers outside,
since it helps hold in moisture.

Chapter Seven

July

Every child is born a naturalist.
His eyes are, by nature,
open to the glories of the stars, the beauty
of the flowers, and the mystery of life.
~ R. Search

"Um . . . No to the pink streaks. They'd look great on Charlotte, though." Darci flipped through the magazine Donovan had bookmarked with her in mind. "I like this one, if we could do a longer version. Chin length would make my face look fatter than it is, and now is not the time to cut back on my donut fetish. I can't let Charlotte snack alone this close to her due date."

"A shorter cut would show off those great cheekbones of yours, but I can go longer if that's what you want." Donovan put the magazine down and picked up his scissors. "So how much can I take off? Two inches?" He indicated the length with his comb, a few inches down from her shoulder.

Darci fidgeted with the stitching on the chair arm, trying to make up her mind. She'd struck up a friendship with Donvan over the past three months, after Wade talked her into taking just a little time for herself. Celia Kemp gave The Hair Dare Your 'Do Salon a rave review in the county paper, but the thing that hooked Darci was listening to the latest gossip as Donovan's fingers worked their magic on her hair, and took her mind off her responsibilities for a while. He'd already talked her into growing out her bangs and she'd gotten a lot of compliments on the caramel streaks he put in a few weeks before.

"It's basically the same style you have now, just a tad shorter, with chunkier layers." Donovan winked at her reflection in the mirror. "Your husband will love it."

"Okay." Darci nodded, but then bit her lip. "But just an inch and a half."

Donovan had just started razoring her layers when an older gentleman came in. He looked familiar as he walked past them toward the back of the salon.

Darci giggled at Donovan's dramatic eye roll.

A girl strutted toward the front door arm-in-arm with the older man. "I might be a little late tomorrow."

"You *did* finish cleaning up, right?" Donovan wore an exasperated expression, but kept his tone even.

"Oh my God," Darci said when the door closed

behind them. "Was that who I think it was? Belinda Blanford and that guy, that Morty who broke up her wedding ceremony?"

"I'm afraid so. Feel sorry for me. Very, very sorry." Donovan shook his head, but the way his eyes were dancing meant he was fixing to give her an earful. "Her dad called in a favor and asked me to hire her when we opened, or trust me, I never would have. At least she's only part time, when she doesn't call in sick."

"I've never seen her cutting hair."

"And you never will." His scissors paused long enough for a dramatic shiver. "She does well to answer the phone and sweep up. I let her shampoo Mrs. Jenkins once and she nearly drowned the poor woman."

"I'm kind of surprised to see she's still running around with ole Morty. Didn't his wife leave him after that scene at the church?"

"Yes, and good for her." Donovan had worked his way to the back of her head after finishing the sides. "But that old guy isn't the only one. Some biker picked her up last week, and I've heard she's seeing Roy Nolan."

"He runs M & N stables now, right?" Darci thought she remembered him from the funeral.

"I believe so, and she's been screwing around with him since before she broke it off with Matthew. Gwen saw her kissing him in front of the stable one day on her way to work. Belinda came in late that day, no big surprise, smelling like pork and vinegar. I remember it was the day after Bradley's birthday, February nineteenth, and her stench didn't go well with my hangover. Anywho, she said she took her boyfriend lunch and one of the boxes leaked on her sweater sleeve. That food smell mixed with her Eau du Ho perfume nearly made me hurl, so I told her to take the rest of the day off."

Donovan gave her a hand mirror. "All done. What do you think?"

"I think I love it!" Darci tousled her hairdo, then pulled a face, pooching her lips out at her reflection. "I bet Wade just might send Paxton to bed early tonight."

On the second Saturday morning in July, Darci sat at the counter listening to Daisy chirp behind her. Sunshine streamed through the windows, splashing the yellow walls with golden rays.

Since Charlotte was due in ten days, Darci insisted she go ahead and start maternity leave. Paxton was out fishing on the Ohio River with Wade and Jimbo. The expectant father-to-be wanted to get in one last fishing trip before he started diaper duty. Paxton latched on to that comment and teased him about 'diaper doo doo duty'.

Hoyt also had the day off but came in around nine to pick up his paycheck. It was a huge relief to Darci when he decided to stay on after graduation. The flexible hours would be perfect for him once community college began in the fall. Hoyt was just about to walk out when the phone rang.

"Hang on a minute, Hoyt," she said, holding up her index finger as she grabbed for the receiver.

"Hey Charlotte, how's it going in Pregger Land?"

Hoyt muttered "uh oh" as Darci felt her eyes widen to the size of flowerpot saucers. He sat down on the stool behind the counter across from where she stood.

"Did you-" Darci paused. "Why didn't-" Darci got up and paced as far as the phone cord allowed. As she walked, she fidgeted with the coiled wire extending from the receiver, alternately wrapping it around her finger and then straightening out a length of it.

"Okay, don't you worry about a thing. Wait a minute." She swung around to face Hoyt. "Don't you dare go anywhere." Then back to the receiver, "Give me five minutes. Don't even move. Just breathe, and be calm. Be very, very calm." She forgot to say goodbye, so she picked up the receiver again, said "bye", then realized how ridiculous that was and muttered "oh, never mind" into the phone before she hung it back up.

"Hey, Boss Lady, you don't look so calm." A poo-eating grin spread across Hoyt's face. It didn't take a genius to figure out a hysterical phone conversation with a pregnant woman could only mean one thing.

"Don't be ridiculous." Darci took a few steps toward the kitchen. She stopped short, then dashed behind the counter to retrieve her purse and car keys instead. "I'm cool as a cucumber. Okay a fried cucumber, but I'm trying. Where the hell are my keys?" Invoices fluttered to the ground as she searched through papers and a pile of raffia.

My work is never done around here. That Darci pretty much knows her stuff, far as plants go, but I still have to step in and help. Like when the boy drowned them chamomile, and those sorry roses. Mercy, those were a sight. Not to mention spikin' Charlotte's tea with all that false unicorn bark and cramp root. She didn't lose the baby, so I reckon it did the trick.

Well, here we go again. I know what's comin' and Miss Darci ain't never gonna make it on time if she has to stop to hunt around for her keys, the ones I see a layin' there on the floor. Fell out of her pocketbook when she pulled out that bar of candy while ago. No wonder she didn't notice, what with her rippin' into it like she hadn't ate in a week. That girl sure does have a sweet tooth. I do believe I made her see me the other night, though. 'Bout time.

All righty, then. I 'bout tired myself out movin' that key ring. I tried to put it by the birdcage, since that little critter sings so pretty every time I go near her and might be able to draw attention over there. Been able to see me from day one, Daisy has, and she's right fond of me, too. I ought to put the notion in Darci's head to get some honeysuckle for her cage. Poor thing gets confused as to why she cain't hop on my hand like she tries, but that just ain't possible. Anyway, I couldn't make it that far, but I put the keys on the table.

Now I just have to find a way to make her notice. Hmmmmm. That just might work. 'This little light of mine, I'm gonna let it shine.' *You like this song, don't you, Daisy girl.* 'O-oh this little light of mine, I'm gonna let it shine, let it shine, let it shine.'

At that moment, a ray of light shined though the porthole and glinted off a crystal vase. The glare in Darci's eyes caught her attention, and she thought it odd that the sun didn't usually come through *that* window this time of morning. Stranger still, she spotted her keys on the display table beside the vase, a place she never cluttered with her personal stuff. She rushed to grab them, only to have them tumble to the floor before she took two more steps.

"So, let me guess. Charlotte must be in labor, huh?" Hoyt picked up the key ring and handed it back to her. She nearly dropped them again as she slung her purse over her shoulder.

"Yep, in a big way. Her water broke a couple minutes ago." Darci put her hands on the counter, palms flat against the cool tile surface, and took a deep breath. "Okay, here's what's going on. Can you, please, please, *please* stay at the store until closing? Sorry, I know it's your day off and under normal circumstances I'd never ask, but I've got to take Charlotte to the hospital and-"

"No problem, I got it covered." Hoyt wasn't miffed at all. His eyes danced as he leaned back against the wall and pulled his shoulder-length hair into a dark ponytail. "I don't have any plans until, like, eight o'clock tonight anyway. Taking Amber to the new sushi place in Evansville."

"Thank you so much! I'll even pay you time and a half," Darci said, relieved she didn't have to close down the shop for the day. "If Wade calls, let him know what's going on and they should be able to figure out where to find us. Jimbo forgot his cell phone, of all things. After aggravating his wife to death before he left this morning, he walks out and leaves his phone on the coffee table. And God forbid Wade take his. His will be turned off on the truck console, in case *he* has an emergency. Damn that Mr. Turner for calling on Wade's day off last year about fixin' his leaky roof. Ever since then, Wade keeps the cell off on weekends, especially when he's out on one of his precious fishing trips."

"You want me to go look for 'em?"

"Thanks, but you'd never be able to track them down. They're somewhere on a stupid little boat on the stupid Ohio River, catching damn stupid little fish." Darci wondered if her irritation showed. "They should be back around lunch. Since first babies usually take their sweet time being born, I'm thinking Baby Villines won't pop out before late this afternoon. Jimbo should have enough time to wash up and be in the delivery room long before that, but you never know. I need to get going."

She trotted toward the door and dropped her keys again. "Damn stupid fishing trip. I'll send Wade over here as soon as I hear from him, but if you haven't heard from us by four, you can go ahead and close up. Yep, shutting down an hour early today would definitely be understandable, I think. See you later." She waved goodbye, opened the door, then bumped into the doorframe.

"Try to drive a little more careful than you're walking," Hoyt said, laughing at her slapstick performance. "Tell Charlotte good luck, or whatever the politically correct thing is to tell a chick who's fixin' to have a baby."

Her hands nearly shook off the steering wheel, but Darci managed to make it to Charlotte's house in one piece. She found her on the couch calmly practicing Lamaze. After she ran out to the trunk with Charlotte's suitcase, which she dropped and tripped over on the way, Darci tried to help her to the car. Charlotte remained on her feet and laughed her ass off when Darci fell off the porch and landed in the grass on the seat of her britches. In spite of all the nervous bumbling, they were on the road in less than three minutes flat.

Webster County was too small to have a hospital of its own, so Charlotte planned to deliver at Henderson Community Methodist Hospital, located twenty minutes from her house in the next county over. She'd already called ahead to let her doctor know she was on the way. Darci kept the Volkswagen Bug between the ditches, despite her hysterics.

"Contraction." Charlotte huffed through the discomfort, but seemed to be holding up pretty well. After a few seconds, she relaxed, her head leaned back against the seat. "Finished. You know, it's really not all that bad."

"Ha! Talk to me when the kid crowns. Then we'll discuss your view of the pain level involved in childbirth. How far apart are the contractions?"

"Don't know exactly. I didn't time 'em, but they're way farther than two minutes," she said, sounding confident. "I know they said in my classes that the two minute mark is when you're usually all the way dilated and the baby could crown."

"You haven't been timing them?" Darci rolled her eyes, then tried to take her voice down a notch from the screech she'd just belted out. "Do you think a little bell in your vagina is gonna start jingling when the baby is ready? Or are you waiting for, perhaps, a little trumpet to poke out of your what-nots to herald the grand arrival?" She couldn't help rolling her eyes again and shook her head. "Terrific. First baby and she doesn't even time the freakin' contractions."

"Okay, so I get your point. I'll time the next one. See, I've got the stopwatch we practiced with." She lifted it to prove she wasn't totally irresponsible. "But you know, those jingle bell things would make it a lot more convenient. Maybe I'll have some installed down there before Jimbo and me get ready for baby number two." She broke down laughing at the sarcastic expression Darci flashed her way.

"I don't know how you're so dang calm. It's not me in labor but I'm a nervous wreck."

"Don't sweat it, Darce. What could possibly go wrong? We're halfway there and the contractions are still pretty . . . uh oh." Charlotte gripped the armrest.

"What the hell does 'uh oh' mean?"

"I'm having another one, the second since we left the house." This was the first sign of worry Charlotte had shown all day. She punched a button on the stopwatch.

"Okay, just do your breathing. That should help." Darci shot a glance at Charlotte. "No, not hold your breath, I said breathing exercises. You know, that huffing and puffing you've been talking about the past four months." Darci puffed her cheeks in and out like a spastic guppy to illustrate. That made her think of fish, which pissed her off. "What kind of idiots would pick today to go fishing, for God's sake? I hope the moron who invented fishing died with a hook up his ass, I tell you what."

Darci's sarcasm and bobbing head made Charlotte laugh again, which apparently hurt her uterus because she grabbed her belly. Then she laughed even harder. Darci broke down and joined her, and felt some of her tension seep away.

Their glee came to a skidding halt, along with

the car whisking them to the hospital.

"What the-" Darci's right arm instinctively flew out to pin Charlotte against the passenger seat, the same reflex she'd have used if Paxton had been riding beside her.

The two women looked at the scene in front of them, then at each other. Confusion and worry played simultaneously in their eyes and across their scrunched foreheads.

Traffic on Highway 41-A stood motionless in front of them. They'd just rolled up on the scene of an accident that couldn't have occurred more than ten minutes before. A truck pulling a cattle trailer blocked the road. From the looks of things, it jackknifed in the act of trying to swerve around a deer on his way across the rural highway. The man Darci assumed to be the driver leaned unharmed against the side of his truck, talking to a highway patrolman. Unfortunately, the deer never made it to the other side of the road, as evidenced by the bloody smear that led to its carcass on the shoulder.

Live cattle wandered everywhere. The end of the trailer faced them in its jackknifed position, the door of which must have been jarred open during the collision. While Darci was thrilled to see the herd alive, all fine and dandy as they mooed on the asphalt, she wondered how the hell she could go about driving around them and the truck. The only alternate route to the hospital would entail using graveled back roads and traveling through the adjacent county to the east, all of which would tack on an hour to their trip to the delivery room. Had the accident not barred their way, they'd be able to make it in about fifteen more minutes.

Every sappy sitcom scenario of babies born in taxicabs on the roadside played through Darci's mind. She groaned, then let loose the most colorful expletive she'd ever used in her life.

A tow truck pulled up beside them, its yellow lights flashing like beacons of hope.

When she turned to Charlotte, she found her expression hard to read. It reminded Darci of when they were about twelve years old at 4-H camp and their counselor caught them smoking her cigarettes. Discovered mid-puff, Charlotte exhaled smoke in the counselor's face and puked on her tennis shoes. Now she had that same look on her face, caught somewhere between wanting to laugh and cry, looking to Darci for a clue as to how they were going to get out of this mess.

Darci willed herself to focus on getting to the hospital instead of on all the things that could go wrong.

"Don't worry. Just try to take deep breaths while I go see what's going on." She hopped out of the car and ran the few yards to speak with the state trooper and the truck driver, where she hastily explained that her pregnant cousin was in labor.

The men exchanged blank looks as they shifted from foot to foot. The driver waved to Charlotte and gave her the thumbs up sign, a big silly grin decorating the features below his cap. The patrolman scooted off to his car, where he could be seen gesturing as he sputtered into his radio. When the tow truck guy walked over, Darci filled him in on why they needed to get the truck, trailer, and cattle off the road as soon as possible. Confused by the situation and the angle of the truck, he lifted his hat and scratched his head. The cows mooed around them.

Darci slid back into the car, her face arranged in an exaggerated display of relief. "Okay, no worries. They should have the trailer moved in a jiffy, then the cop is gonna give us an escort to the hospital, flashing lights, siren, and the whole shebang." In her mind, Darci imagined what she'd like Jimbo to do with his fishing pole.

The semi had come to a stop on its side of the road, so moving the trailer that swung around even with the cab was the main objective. The men, thinking much more quickly than Darci would have thought possible, unhooked the trailer and had it towed out of the way a couple minutes later. The next problem to tackle would be the cattle that stood huddled like witless statues on both sides of the yellow line. As the driver tried unsuccessfully to shoo them into the left lane, Darci let loose another expletive.

"Oh hell." Charlotte grabbed her tummy with one hand and the stopwatch with the other, huffing through the contraction.

"How far apart are they now?" Darci fidgeted with the seatbelt, since it was the only thing she found to grab.

"Um." Charlotte winced apologetically. "About eight minutes."

"Good. We've still got plenty of time," Darci said, her voice full of confidence she didn't feel. "Nothing to worry about." She sat there for three endless seconds that seemed like a decade. "I'll be right back. Don't move."

Charlotte reverted to her normal personality. "Well, I had planned to hike through the woods, then maybe go bareback bronco riding on one of those bulls, but fine. For you, I'll sit still."

Darci jumped out and trotted to where the men stood discussing how to move a few thousand pounds of walking sirloin out of the way.

Tow Truck Guy asked the semi driver, "Why cain't you move your own cattle outta the way, man? They ain't listenin' to you a' tall."

"These ain't my damn cows. I just get paid to drive 'em wherever the man who owns 'em tells me to."

Oh, good grief, Darci thought. Easy to tell these three were a bunch of city boys. The last thing she needed. She realized she'd have to take care of the situation herself, and the time she'd spent on her grandparents' farm flooded through her memory.

Darci moved at a steady though not too fast pace toward the cattle. "Y'all stand across the road with your arms out like this," she instructed the men, her voice ringing with authority she didn't know she possessed. They mimicked her airplane arms, following in a horizontal line behind her, and exchanged looks that said they hoped she knew what she was doing.

"No sudden moves, just don't let 'em get

around you." Darci knew she couldn't second guess herself now, with Charlotte about to give birth in the car. "Let's just try to move 'em off the road into the bean field."

Most of the cattle moved in the direction Darci wanted, possibly eyeing the fresh soybean plants that must have looked like a bovine buffet to them. One big steer wasn't so eager, though. He mooed and nodded his head up and down in warning, his eyes glued to the people coming toward him with outstretched arms.

Intimidated, the three man army behind Darci slowed to a stop.

"Oh, for God's sake! It's not like he's gonna bite you or run you through like in a bullfight cartoon." Darci stomped her foot in frustration, which the steer didn't seem to appreciate. "Come on, back me up here."

The nervous bunch followed her lead. Soon the small herd moved off the road and into the field. The way her day was going, Darci expected the owner of the crop to show up any minute and hand her a bill for whatever the cows ate, tromped over, or shit on.

She tried to scrape a mound of cow poop off her shoe as she opened the car door. "The cop is moving his car in front of us, then we'll follow him to the hospital. Yuck." The greenish black manure wasn't coming off too easily. "Just a minute." She ran to the trunk, where she kept a pair of orange rubber boots. She chucked her sneakers in, slammed the trunk shut, then hopped back in the driver's seat wearing bright tangerine footwear with her jeans.

"What does he want now?" Charlotte directed Darci's attention to the truck driver on his way to the passenger side window. It looked like he had a bunch of weeds tucked under one arm.

"What the hell?" Darci said, her finger on the button to let down the window.

"These are for you, little lady." He handed Charlotte a bouquet of wild honeysuckle that grew on the roadside, tied together with a red bandana. The scent from the yellow and white blooms masked the smell of cow manure that wafted up through the trunk. "Sorry about the holdup."

"Oh, that's so sweet," Charlotte said, burying her nose in the flowers. Darci tromped the gas pedal then, so she had to yell the rest of her thanks through the window as the green Volkswagen sped off behind the squad car. The guy was still waving, the last sight they had of him in the rearview mirror.

Charlotte's contractions were even closer together when they pulled under the emergency room canopy. Darci waved to the policeman, shouting her thanks as she helped Charlotte waddle inside. She handed her over to a nurse, then sprinted back out to park the car and bring in the Lamaze bag.

Jimbo, to Darci's extreme relief, skittered into ER just as a maternity nurse was about to wheel Charlotte down to delivery. Darci kissed the mother-to-be on the forehead, then reminded her she'd be in the waiting room if she needed anything.

Darci found Wade and Paxton there waiting for her.

"Hi Hon." Wade put his arm around her shoulder when she fell into the chair beside him. Paxton seemed engrossed in some animated show on the television, which he watched until he dozed off. "I saw the missed call on my cell when we got back to the pickup, and when I called Petal Pushers, Hoyt told me the news. We got here as quick as we could. How's Charlotte?"

"She's fine, but I'm amazed how fast things are moving, especially since it took me eighteen hours of hard labor to deliver Paxton. Charlotte's water broke around nine this morning and now she's fully dilated just four hours later. It's a good thing she didn't sneeze in the car, 'cause I'm thinking the baby would've squirted out if she had."

While they waited for news, Wade tried to break the silence. "You wanna hear about the big bass I hauled in with that new lure I ordered off eBay?"

Darci had just opened her mouth to tell him exactly what she thought about his fishing trip when Jimbo bounced into the room.

"It's a boy!" Decked out in green delivery scrubs, Jimbo grinned from ear to ear.

They headed to the nursery to wait beside the window for a peek at the baby. Everyone cooed like idiots, their faces pressed against the glass, when a nurse put him in a little bed that looked like an aquarium on wheels.

His little pink head, crowned with a fluffy blue hat she knew Jimbo's mom had knitted for him, was the only part of the baby they could see. A yellow and green striped blanket, which matched the others in the nursery, was wrapped snuggly around the infant.

"Oh, look at his teensy little hand." Darci pointed to the miniature pink arm the baby boy worked free from his blankie.

"That's gonna be his pitching arm," Jimbo bragged. He gave Paxton a playful punch on the shoulder. "Think he'll be ready for battin' practice next week?"

Paxton offered up a forced grin, but his mother saw him look at Jimbo as if he thought his cousin-in-law belonged on the floor with the mental patients.

"Did y'all decide on a name yet?" Darci hoped Jimbo hadn't convinced Charlotte to name him after his grandpa Bertram.

Jimbo beamed as he introduced his son. "We named the little man Cole Thomas Villines. Cute but macho, don't ya think?"

Petal Pushers' Plant of the Month for July
is

Honeysuckle
Lonicera x heckrottii
Vine

Common name: Woodbine and Trumpet Honeysuckle.

Brief description: The vines can grow twelve to twenty feet, with pink and yellow tubular flowers that attract hummingbirds and butterflies. A few varieties are scentless, but Pink Lemonade honeysuckle (*Lonicera x heckrottii*) and wild honeysuckle, with white and yellow flowers, and most others have a deliciously sweet scent.

Symbolism: the bond of love.

Trivia: Want to taste honeysuckle? Here's a trick most kids from Webster County could show you. Pick a fresh honeysuckle flower and hold the end between the thumb and index finger of your left hand. Pinch off the base of the flower with your other hand and it pull it and the stamen, slowly and carefully, out through the bottom. You'll see a bead of nectar. One taste will let you know why the bees and hummingbirds flock to it.

Growing instructions: Honeysuckle grows well in full sun or partial shade, and should be pruned as needed. They spread quickly and can be invasive, but it's pure heaven to smell honeysuckle when you walk past it on a summer day.

Uses: These can grow along a fence, on an arbor or trellis, and up the side of buildings. Honeysuckle works well as a cut flower, so mix some in with your wildflower bouquets.

Tools & Tips: Everyone should take advantage of the local garden tours going on this time of year. This is a terrific way to learn how to incorporate different plants into your landscape, meet fellow gardeners from your area, and pick up all kinds of new ideas. There's no better way to spend a sunny afternoon.

Daisy, the little parakeet you've probably seen helping me at Petal Pushers, is a fan of this plant. I bring in springs of honeysuckle to put in her cage, and she loves to tweet away perched on it.

Grandma Odette's Famous Hummingbird Cake

My Grandma Odette's been on my mind lately, so as an added bonus this month, I thought I'd include her recipe for Hummingbird Cake. Let her know how much you love it the next time you see her.

Ingredients:
3 cups all-purpose flour
2 cups sugar
1 teaspoon baking soda
1 teaspoon salt
1 teaspoon ground cinnamon
3 large eggs
1 cup canola oil
1-1/2 teaspoon vanilla extract
1 8-ounce can crushed pineapple, with the liquid
1 cup chopped pecans
2 cups mashed ripe bananas
Cream Cheese Icing (recipe below)
(Optional) ½ cup chopped pecans
(Optional) edible flowers (nasturtiums, honeysuckle, or even squash blossoms, just be sure the ones you use are safe to eat)

Instructions:

1. With a big wooden spoon, mix together flour, sugar, baking soda, salt, and cinnamon. Add the eggs, oil, and vanilla, stirring until the batter is moist. Gently fold in the undrained pineapple, bananas, and pecans.

2. Grease and flour two or three round cake pans, your choice, and divide the batter between them. Bake at 350 degrees for twenty-five to thirty minutes, or until a toothpick poked in the middle comes out clean.

3. Cool for ten minutes before removing from the pans.

4. When completely cool, ice the layers with cream cheese frosting. Put extra pecans around the edge and arrange a few edible flowers on the top.

5. Keep refrigerated.

Cream Cheese Icing

Ingredients:
8 ounces of cream cheese, softened
½ cup margarine, softened
16-oz bag of powdered sugar, sifted
1 teaspoon vanilla extract

Instructions:

1. With an electric mixer, beat together the cream cheese and margarine until smooth.

2. Gradually add the powdered sugar until light and fluffy, then add the vanilla.

Chapter Eight

August

*We can complain because rose bushes have
thorns, or rejoice because thorn bushes
have roses.*
~ Abraham Lincoln

On her weekly visit to Golden Days Retirement
Home, Darci wondered why she couldn't find
more to do. The thin application of mulch around
the bushes prevented grass from sprouting
through, but she expected to see at least a few
stray dandelions in the border, and found it
strange that not a single weed infringed the tidy
flowerbed. She deadheaded some of the older
rosebushes, snipping off wilting blooms to encourage new ones to form in their place, then decided to check on the herbs.

It wasn't necessary for her to come by as often
as she did, but since the building was located in

the middle of town and everyone knew Petal Pushers tended the landscaping, she wanted to keep the grounds in pristine condition. Word of mouth was free advertising, after all. The other reason she enjoyed stopping by was the conversation. Most of the people who lived there were vivacious and lively, eager to talk to her about everything from flowers to fashion to the latest antics of some the more risqué residents.

Bernice gossiped with Darci while she sat on the sidewalk pinching back herbs. "Edith Wilson coming to the cafeteria in her slip was the buzz until yesterday. Edward Johansson got irritated with the attendant who brought him a diuretic, a medication he thought he didn't need and ought not have to take. Well, to prove his point, Ole Eddy unzipped his fly and took a whiz all over the male nurse's white shoes. That wasn't half as shocking as what he told the man to do." Bernice lowered her voice to a temporary whisper. "Eddy told him, in less polite words than I'm gonna repeat, to go fornicate with himself! He sure did. Then, while the poor guy's shoes were still dripping pee, the old cuss offered to let him use his walker." Bernice shook her head and laughed.

"I'm almost afraid to ask, but why would somebody on staff need to use his walker?"

"Oh, he didn't *need* it, but Eddy gave him a vivid description of something that sounded mighty uncomfortable for him to do with it!" Bernice winked and slapped her knee. "I'll tell you what, sweetie, there's nary a dull moment under this roof."

One morning not long after, Wade's assistant took a load of lumber to a job site on the other side of town. The company truck being Wade's only vehicle, he asked Darci for a lift to work.

The sky was a beautiful shade of golden pink, a few fluffy cumulus clouds adding soft texture to nature's canvas as Darci drove Wade down Main Street. As they approached Golden Days, she caught sight of something that brought her VW Bug to a screeching halt in front of the retirement home. Wade muttered a few choice words when the steaming hot coffee from his spill proof travel mug sloshed onto his crotch.

Mabel Guthrie maneuvered her cane at a surprising pace as she dashed across the lawn. Her damaged left arm flailed as if threatening some unseen adversary, and she appeared to be charging the flowers that bordered the building.

Darci threw open the car door and jumped out, unsure whether Mrs. Guthrie was being chased or attacking the foliage. She kicked off her sandals as she sprinted across the dewy yard, damp bits of grass sticking to her feet as she zipped toward Mabel. How the hell could a woman that old who'd suffered a debilitating stroke move so fast? Darci heard Mabel holler as she shortened the distance between them.

"Scat!" Mabel hissed. "Git!"

Two squirrels, who looked as if they were scared half out of their furry little wits, darted out from behind a large clump of monkey grass that grew in the border along the front of the retirement home. In their escape, they ran twin spirals up an oak tree at the edge of the property, then disappeared amongst acorns and bird nests high in its leafy boughs.

Darci looked back toward Mabel, who still had no idea anyone stood a few feet behind her. "Look. Wha. You. Did." She shook her head as she limped toward the flowerbed.

Mabel stepped into the border and carefully placed her feet between the ruby red impatiens. Darci restrained herself from rushing over as Mabel eased herself steadily to the ground, her cane supporting her as she slid down the wall. She saw the determination in her eyes, plus she wanted to see what she planned to do.

In a seated position, Mrs. Guthrie shook her head as she smoothed out the piles of mulch the pesky critters had been digging in. With her functional right hand, she picked up an impatiens one of the little buggers uprooted, carefully removed a few damaged leaves, then replanted it in the hole from which the bushytailed squirrels had ripped it.

"Is everything all right, Mrs. Guthrie," Darci asked, bending down beside her. She remembered her request to be addressed by her first name and amended, "I mean Miss Mabel." The citizens of Webster County still went by the time honored Southern tradition of using 'Miss' for older women who deserved respect, if calling them by their first name.

Mabel's head came up when Darci spoke. Elbow deep in mulch and red flowers, she looked a bit embarrassed, as if she'd been caught doing something she shouldn't. "Sorry. Squirrels. Messed. Your. Flowers. Up. Didn't. Mean. Bother. Your-"

"I saw those little farts running off when I came up." Under normal circumstances, Darci would never interrupt Mabel or anyone else intentionally. But seeing how laborious long sentences were for her, and since she saved the border plants from the damn rodents, she thought this interruption was for the best.

"Thank you so much for fixing up the mess they made!" Mabel had indeed put everything in the border back to rights, even smoothing the mulch back over the dirt and tossing the leaves that had fallen off. If Darci hadn't witnessed what happened minutes before, she would never have known anything had been amiss. "You certainly didn't have to, but you did a great job of it."

Darci helped the older woman up, then the two stepped out of the plant bed. Darci followed her to the bench nearest them.

"Not. Mad?" Mabel appeared worried that she might have overstepped her bounds or gotten in her way somehow.

"Of course not. Shoot, you just saved me a lot of work. I appreciate it."

As they sat there, Darci noticed that Wade had moved her car to an actual parking space near the curb. She could see him reading the paper in the front seat, obviously not planning to rush her. Being his own boss had its perks, like not getting yelled at if he showed up a few minutes late.

"So. Glad. To. Help." Mabel's radiant face brightened an already beautiful morning. The ruby throated hummingbird fluttering around the roses behind their bench added to the magic.

It suddenly became quite clear to Darci why there hadn't been any weeds to pull. "Do you come out this early every morning?"

"Yes." Mabel nodded. "Early riser. All my life." Her speech seemed to flow a little quicker as her comfort level rose.

"You know, Hoyt and me had just about convinced ourselves we had garden fairies, sprites or whatever they're called, since this place hasn't needed much tending."

Mabel glanced sheepishly at her shoes, then peered up through dancing blue eyes. A grin twisted the right side of her mouth.

"You've been pulling all those weeds for us, haven't you?" Darci was overcome by admiration for Mabel, amazed by the things she accomplished in the early morning hours all by herself. The exercises her doctors told her to do, Mabel most likely thought of as silly and frivolous; gardening was good honest work, something that obviously made her feel useful.

Mabel nodded. "Love flowers. Always. Gardening, is fun." She gazed at Darci, pleading with her eyes. "Alright to. Keep on. Helping? Please."

"Of course it's alright, Miss Mabel." Darci patted Mabel's elbow and struggled to blink back the tears tickling her ducts. "And you don't have to ask me if it's okay. You live here, for goodness sake, and seem to be doing a better job than I could. Please keep on doing anything you like."

Wade rolled down the window when Darci glanced his way, a smirk on his face as he pointed to his watch. She waved to him, then said her goodbyes to Mabel.

When she arrived at the shop that morning, Darci decided it would be a good idea to call Golden Days Retirement Home. Even though Mabel seemed perfectly safe alone, she thought she should let someone in charge know about her habit of venturing outside early each morning. She dialed the number, but felt like a big tattletale and disconnected the call twice before letting it ring.

"I appreciate your calling, but I'm already aware of Mrs. Guthrie's activities." Vera Thompkins' jovial voice made Darci glad she'd dialed the phone. "You see, since many residents keep odd hours, either rising with the chickens or staying up playing solitaire all night, nurses make rounds twenty-four hours a day to keep an eye on everybody. I'm so glad to hear that her gardening doesn't bother you. Some people would've thought she was just some old busybody trying to interfere with your job."

"Oh, I don't feel that way at all. I just wanted to let you know she was out and about that early, well, just so maybe you could look out every now and then, in case she overexerts herself or anything."

"You don't have to worry about Mrs. Guthrie," Mrs. Tompkins assured her. "Since she started working with the plants a few weeks ago, you simply wouldn't believe how much she's come out of her shell. The partial paralysis made her very self-conscious about the way she moved and spoke. In the fourteen or so months she's lived with us, she kept to herself. Hardly ever said a word, except when her family came to visit."

"Oh, that's so sad. The few times I've been around her, it's been easy to see she's still full of life." The lady Darci saw chasing squirrels up a tree this morning certainly wasn't ready for a rocking chair in some dark corner.

"But that's just it. These past few weeks, Mrs. Guthrie is a new person. The yard work seems to give her confidence. Bernice-always into everything Bernice, God bless her-caught her pulling weeds one morning. I think the time sort of got away from Mabel that day, since she used to stop around seven to keep from being noticed. Anyway, Bernice told some of the others what had 'lit the fire under Mabel's butt', as she put it. When people start talking to her about gardening and things, she seems to forget herself and loosens up a bit."

"That's good to know, that she's feeling better and letting herself make friends." Darci smiled, imagining Mabel schmoozing with the other folks she'd met at Golden Days.

"She had a doctor's appointment last week and he couldn't believe the progress she's made. Her speech is getting a little faster, and the extra talking seems to help her facial muscles, too. Her limp hasn't improved, but she's gained a bit of mobility in her left hand. She's always been able to move her arm, she just didn't have much control over it. Now her wrist is more flexible and she can wiggle her fingers. The physical improvements are wonderful, but it's the social progress that I'm most happy about. She used to stay in her bedroom after supper each night, wouldn't join in the evening activities. Now she's a night owl and watches television in the common room. I think *Chelsea Lately* is her favorite, if you can believe it."

"Well, she does seem awful spunky." Darci chuckled at the idea of proper Miss Mabel watching the racy late night talk show.

"And she's joining in other activities, as well." Pride rang through Mrs. Tompkins' voice. "She interacts with some of the volunteers and plays checkers. And you would *not* believe the beautiful sewing she does with our quilting circle. Her left hand is just mobile enough to hold a thimble under the quilt top and push the needle back up. Her right hand is as talented at stitching as it ever was. You'll have to come take a look at the gorgeous engagement ring quilt the ladies are working on."

Darci did just that when she popped by during the middle of the afternoon on her way back from picking up supplies. Mabel, Bernice, and about six other people sat clustered around the television watching *General Hospital*. The ladies hardly took their eyes off the set, elbowing each other when Luke conned the Quartermaines and blushing during Sonny's love scene. After the soap opera went off, the quilters were more than happy to show her their latest project.

The quilt was exquisite enough to hang in a gallery, but Darci thought Mabel Guthrie was the most beautiful thing in the room. Standing in the center of her friends, she smiled with the unparalyzed half of her face. The left side seemed to move just a bit more than the last time she'd seen her. Darci hoped it was from all the smiling.

"Aaargh!"

"What the hell is wrong?" Startled out of a sound sleep, Wade sent the alarm clock clattering to the floor when he reached for the lamp on the nightstand.

The light helped Darci orient herself. She sat up in bed hugging her pillow. Sweat plastered her bangs to her forehead.

"Sorry, I just had a bad dream. Go back to sleep."

Wade gave her a kiss on the cheek, then turned off the lamp. "Night, Hon. Sweet dreams."

With the covers around her shoulders, she snuggled her back up next to Wade to remind herself she wasn't alone. She tried to go back to sleep, but blurred fragments of her strange dream crept through her thoughts. There was a coffin with horses walking around it, big red leaves scattered underneath, a jar of bacon fat, and a man wearing a dress and bright pink blusher.

"Oh my God." Darci bolted out of bed, pulling

on her housecoat as she hurried downstairs. "Ricin, castor plant, mole beans . . . . That has to be it."

Seated in the recliner, she snatched up a book from the coffee table and opened it to the page bookmarked with a Hershey's candy bar wrapper. Her finger skimmed the paragraphs underneath color pictures of a plant with the genus species *Ricinus communis*. Castor plant was the name of the leafy vegetation she'd seen when she took the level to Wade at his work site. It grew four to six feet in height and flourished in full sun, with maroon-tinted leaves that consisted of five to nine lobes. People set the toxic plants, commonly known as mole bean, in areas of their yard plagued by pests. The beans, also referred to as seeds, held the most concentrated level of poison, but one nibble on any part of the plant, and the mole, shrews, or any other living thing would drop deader than a doornail. The picture of the plant's seeds, about the size of a dime, reminded Darci of big fat ticks.

Under the 'uses' subheading, she learned the laxative called castor oil came from the mole bean plant. The word 'caution' printed in bold red letters drew her attention, and she gasped when she found what she'd jumped out of her cozy bed to look for. The volume urged people with small children and pets not to plant *Ricinus communis* on their property, since ingesting even a small piece of any part of the plant could be fatal.

She read the next sentence out loud. "The poison, known as ricin, is similar in molecular structure to anthrax, is one thousand times deadlier than cobra venom, and has no known antidote." Her voice seemed to echo in the quiet room, which spooked her even more.

Darci fidgeted with the sash on her robe, rolling and unrolling the end into a ball, and mulled over the significance of what she'd just read. After a while, she went to the kitchen and took an antihistamine; she wasn't having an allergic reaction to anything, but knew swallowing the pill was the only way she'd get back to sleep. It looked like tomorrow was going to be a busy day.

Darci pushed the doorbell, then stood back waiting for the door to open. She shifted the paper bag of extra cabinet knobs she'd asked Wade for this morning, when she explained she needed an excuse to drop by Mrs. Nolan's to ask for some plant clippings. Of course she hadn't bothered to tell him exactly why she needed them, since she didn't have time to listen to a lecture about minding her own business.

"Good morning." Teresa Nolan opened the door, a smile on her face and a mixing bowl in her hands. She continued stirring but elbowed the door open further. "Come on in, Darci."

"Sorry to bother you, I can see you're busy with your baking and all, but Wade asked me to drop off these leftover pieces for your kitchen cabinets." Darci followed her into the kitchen and placed the bag on the counter. Her nose twitched right before her stomach growled. The scent of chocolate cupcakes Teresa Nolan pulled out of the oven reminded her that she'd skipped breakfast.

"Thank you. You never know when you'll need spare parts." Teresa iced a cupcake that had been cooling on the rack, then held it out to her unexpected guest. "Here, I could use a taste tester."

"Um, tank oo," Darci mumbled through the huge bite in her mouth. The chocolate cupcake with cherry icing was heaven to her taste buds. "Delicious." She swallowed. "While I'm here, I wanted to ask you if it would be alright if I took a few cutting from your yard."

"I could probably do you one better." Teresa beamed with pride. Like most gardeners, she was more than happy to share the fruits of her labor of love. "I've collected seeds for years, so tell me which plants you like, and I'll fix you right up." She pulled a cardboard box from a cabinet under the sink, then took the lid off to show hundreds of plastic baggies, each neatly labeled. Some held tiny specks, others whole dried pods.

"I wish I was this organized." Darci's fingers glided over the baggies, lost for a minute in some of the rare flower varieties she saw. "That plant with the big reddish leaves has been on my mind since the last time I was here, the one with the spiked pods. And I'd love some of these Chinese House seeds, too, if you could spare a few."

"Big red leaves," Teresa said, thinking. "Oh, you mean my mole beans! Sure, I've got a lot of those. It's fun to trade seeds, and I've sold some on eBay when I get bored in the winter." She took a larger bag from the edge of the box. "I'm sure you know, but these are easy as pie to grow. My dad used to just drop 'em in holes in the yard to get rid of moles and such. The plants just pretty much take care of themselves. Here you go." She handed Darci an envelope she'd just filled with seeds similar to dried pinto beans, along with another that contained the other seeds she asked about, plus a few four o'clocks Teresa threw in.

On the way back to the front door, Darci decided to ask a question, and hoped she wouldn't stick her foot in her mouth. "Are your kids and their girlfriends seeds collectors too?"

"No, but I'm hoping to train a grandbaby to, whenever my son finds a nice girl to settle down with. If that ever happens." Teresa raised her eyebrows. "The ones he goes for only care about collecting clothes and jewelry."

The phone rang in the Nolan home just as Darci stepped outside, her morning mission accomplished. Seeds worked out even better than clippings, since they'd keep better, plus show which plants had been on the property for at least a few years. She couldn't wait to show Max.

She sent him a quick text before she pulled out of Teresa's driveway, to ask him to swing by Petal Pushers when he got off work. Her phone beeped with his reply a few minutes later, but she waited to read it until after she parked beside her shop.

'Love 2, but I'm busier than a one legged

man in a butt kickin contest. :) Rain check til day after tomorrow?'

Well, it looked like she'd have to wait to tell him her news, but that might not be a bad thing. She could mull over the facts and make sure her hunch was right before she spoke with him. Last thing she wanted to do was stir up a stink, pointing fingers at innocent people because she let her imagination run wild, though she was pretty dang sure that wasn't the case.

'Sure thing.' Darci's thumbs pecked across her phone's qwerty keyboard. 'Don't work too hard. Tell Mae hi for me. Love, Darci'

That afternoon, the printer spit out some papers as Darci logged off the computer. She took them from the tray, tapped the bottom edges on her desk to straighten the stack, then tucked them in the bottom drawer beside the envelope full of seeds Teresa gave her earlier.

After she stood up and stretched, still sleepy from being up half the night before, Darci spotted Paxton's mitt in the corner of the shop, right where he'd left it between yesterday's Little League practice and fishing with his dad. When she picked it up, a baseball nestled inside plopped out and rolled across her foot.

She ran her fingertips over the rawhide stitching. Paxton spent a few minutes the night before each game polishing his glove with the neem oil his coach recommended. The boy convinced himself that if he skipped this ritual, they'd lose for sure. Each win meant free ice cream from the coach, with three in a row guaranteeing a pizza deliveryman would show up after the game, toting cheese and pepperoni pies for the whole team. Darci thought it was cute, and realized she was lucky Paxton didn't copy some of the stranger quirks from the big league guys, like not changing his underwear when they were on a winning streak. She shuddered, imagining the nastiness of two-week-old underwear on a pack of little boys. Yuck. She slipped the mitt onto her hand and tossed the ball into it.

Hoyt walked in through the side door. He'd been out making deliveries, but grinned when he noticed the sports equipment. "Gearing up for a ball game, Boss Lady?"

"Not exactly." Darci giggled at the thought of her clumsy self on a baseball diamond, fumbling the ball each time she touched it. "Paxton forgot this when he left. Here, catch. And don't call me Boss Lady." She pitched him an underhanded toss, which he easily caught.

Hoyt pitched it back to her, apparently forgetting she had no sports skills whatsoever. The phone rang as the ball slid out of his grip, rocketing to the place where his boss had stood until she moved to answer the ring. "Uh oh." The ball crunched into the wall. Darci made a shushing motion when he tried to get her attention, so he trudged over and inspected the damage.

The ball was stuck in the drywall. When Hoyt touched it, it fell through to the inside, where it

154

bounced a few times, ricocheting off the beams before coming to a rest.

"Damn, it's cold in here." Hoyt rubbed his bare arms, then crossed the floor to check the thermostat. "Hey, I think this thing's broke," he said, but Darci frowned and shushed him again. He shrugged, but waited for her to get off the phone.

"Um, sorry about that." He pointed toward the wall when she finished jotting down the order and sat the pencil down on the counter beside her notepad.

"Eww." Darci's face matched Hoyt's wince. "Guess we're both grounded, huh." She took a deep breath, reminding herself she slept with the carpenter who'd be fixing the hole. Lucky to dodge an added out-of-pocket expense, she smiled at Hoyt, then noticed he wore the same wide-eyed frown Paxton did when he knew he was in trouble. "Kidding! It was my fault anyway, so don't look so worried. Wade can fix this the next time he has a few free minutes. We'll just cover it up until then."

She reached under the counter to pick up the previous month's copy of her favorite gardening magazine and a pair of scissors. "I know just the perfect camouflage." She flipped through the glossy pages until she came to a full-page photograph of an English knot garden, then snipped it out and placed it face down in front of her. She looped Scotch tape into little circles to function as double-sided adhesive, which she put in each corner, smoothed the pin-up over the hole, then turned to Hoyt. "Voila. Nobody will be the wiser."

She called to Hoyt again before he walked out back to water the vegetable slips. "We might not ought to mention how this happened in front of Paxton. I sort of have a rule about not playing ball inside, and I don't want to give the boy any excuse to break it."

"No problem. I got your back." Hoyt winked and pointed to her with both index fingers. "As far as I'm concerned, I don't know anything except that hole was a work related mishap."

"Way to cover for your boss there, Hoyt."

Bright and early the next morning, Darci muttered a few choice words as she stomped across the yard to the outdoor display set up on the porthole side of the shop. As she drove up to Petal Pushers, she'd noticed the upside down flowerpots that were supposed to be on top of the straw bales, the cute Back to School sign she made from an old chalkboard now cattywampus on the ground between them.

Hand on hip, she shook her head at the mess. The last storm blew through days ago, and the slight summer breeze that barely moved the leaves overhead was far too weak to budge full terra cotta pots. Probably just some kids' bad idea of a prank, or maybe a few damn drunken morons couldn't find anything better to do last night.

Darci squatted down, her fingers sifting through the potting soil to see if she could salvage the hydrangeas and marigolds squashed underneath. Bells jingling from the front door drew her attention. Not the best time for a customer, but sales took precedence over cleanup any day.

The only plant that still sat on the straw was about half a foot from her head. The second she moved to stand, the flowerpot exploded. Bits of dirt and terra cotta hit the right side of her face and arm.

Too stunned to scream, frozen in place, she turned to stare at the broken pot. Maybe she had somehow managed to royally piss off the Ghost Lady and this was the poltergeist version of a hissy fit. She dismissed that idea when something pinged behind her as it bit a chunk out of the siding.

A scream left her mouth before she realized she was running full speed toward the front door.

Hoyt heard her holler and rushed up front from the work room, where he'd been busy breaking down boxes from a recent shipment of floral supplies. "What's wrong? I-"

"Shit on a biscuit, get down!" Darci locked the deadbolt and dove for cover under the counter, yanking Hoyt along with her. "Some fool's shooting at me!" Remembering the jingle, she poked her head out far enough so she could scan the room. "Where'd the customer go? I don't know if insurance'll cover somebody getting shot in here." Her hands cupped around her mouth, she yelled, "Duck and cover, wherever you are. We're under attack!"

"Nobody came in yet, Boss Lady." Hoyt accomplished a near impossible facial expression; he frowned, brows raised over widened eyes. "You *sure* somebody shot at you?" Why was he staring at her face like that?

"Yes I'm sure, and don't call me that. Would I ever in my right mind close the shop during business hours if it wasn't an emergency? Oh hell, I've gotta lock the back door. Don't move."

Before he could say anything, Darci skittered to the rear door and back on her hands and knees.

"Hand me the phone, just don't stand up all the way in front of the window. He could think it's me and shoot you, and I won't have you getting hurt." Her voice broke on the last words.

She made it a policy never to call Max while he was on duty, afraid to interrupt him in the middle of some important police work. An email or text she knew he wouldn't answer if he was busy, so that was fine. Normally. Today was an emergency.

Her godfather picked up on the second ring.

Sirens blared and blue lights flashed as Max arrived minutes later.

Hoyt let him in. Darci remained huddled under the counter. Her hands, fingers laced together, still protectively covered her head. She knew she must look like one of those people in a bomb shelter ad from the fifties, not that she gave a damn.

"You okay, Darce?" Max squatted down so he could see her. "Come on out so I can get a better look at you, make sure you're all in one piece."

"He's trying to shoot me." She shook her head. "Might be a good idea to stay under here for a while."

"Everything's gonna be alright. The shooter's long gone by now." Max extended his hand toward her. "Got a deputy by both your doors and a couple more checking out the tree line where you think the shots came from. I won't let anybody get you."

Darci took his hand and stood up facing him, her shoulders hunched.

"Hoyt, what say you make us some coffee." Max's soothing voice calmed Darci's nerves. "Pull the shades in the kitchen, if you don't mind, just to make us all feel a little safer. And find me some Band-aids. We'll be there in a minute."

"Sure thing, Sheriff."

"Now, let's see how bad you're hurt." Max tucked a strand of hair behind her right ear, then turned her chin to the left. His brow puckered, then he smoothed his face into a reassuring expression she'd seen many times as a kid, usually after she fell off her bike or found some other clumsy way to hurt herself.

"They missed, so I'm fine. Just shook up."

"Uh huh." He dabbed her forehead and cheek with his handkerchief, which he then balled up and tucked quickly back in his pocket. He poked a few keys on his cell phone, said numbers that made no sense to Darci, and put it back in his belt case. "Your arm got scratched up, see," he said, gently touching the area above her elbow.

"Must be from when the flowerpot exploded." Dirt specks dotted her arm. At least it didn't look bad, just a few scratches, like he said.

"There's a little gash on your cheek too, right here." He plucked a Kleenex from the desk and dabbed her forehead again. This time she saw red stuff on it before he hid it in his pocket. "Nothing to worry about, though."

"*Little* gash?" The room started to spin. "You sure it's not a bullet hole?"

Max opened his arms and the next thing she knew, she was crying into his chest. The blood smear on his shirt when she pulled away made her queasy, but the tears took away some of the panic. She was going to be okay.

He led the way to the kitchen table, pulled out a chair for her, and stuck a bandage on her forehead before her butt hit the cushioned seat. The overhead light was on, since the shades blocked out the sunshine, and Hoyt had steaming cups of coffee for each of them.

"Now let's get down to business." Max took a memo pad from his shirt pocket, clicked his ink pen, then asked Darci and Hoyt to go over everything that happened that morning.

"So neither of you heard gunfire?" Both shook their heads as Max looked back over his notes. "Guy must've used a silencer. Okay. Now, you have any idea who pulled the trigger? Has anybody threatened you?"

"Nobody's threatened me, but . . ." Darci fidgeted with her napkin, twisting it into a thin rope she wound around her finger. "I have a pretty good idea who shot at me. It has to do with what I wanted to talk to you about when I texted you yesterday."

"Oh Darci, if you were in some kind of trouble all you had to do was say so. I'd've dropped everything in a heartbeat."

"I know, but I wasn't one hundred percent sure, and I wanted to think things over before I told you who I thought was responsible for Cyril Maldonado's murder."

"Murder? We pretty much chalked his death up to accidental poisoning." Max rubbed his freshly shaven chin. "What did you get yourself in to?"

She sent Hoyt to go get the seed envelope and papers from her desk drawer while she filled the sheriff in on her suspicions, starting with her midnight epiphany after her nightmare and the research on castor plants. When Hoyt plunked down the seed packet, she told Max about going to see Teresa Nolan the day before.

"The phone rang right as I left. Probably Roy, which is why I think he's the one who tried to kill me this morning." She shuddered, then took a sip of coffee. "Teresa must have told him about my visit, and about the seeds she gave me. Plus, his girlfriend Belinda could've heard Donovan tell me about the day in February when she came in smelling like bacon grease and vinegar. That's why he'd think I figured the whole thing out."

"I'm not quite following you on the smelly girl." Max jotted something down in his notes, then flipped back a few pages. "That'd be Belinda Blanford, but what exactly does her bad hygiene have to do with this?"

"She works at the hair salon. Donovan's friend Gwen saw Belinda hanging all over Roy by the stables, which is why she got to work late that day. Donovan was hungover because he'd celebrated Bradley's birthday the night before, on the nineteenth. He sent Belinda home because he was already mad about her being late again, but the smell made him gag. She said she took lunch to her boyfriend and spilled some on her sweater. I don't know if she's in on the murder, but I think she must've brought Roy takeout from the diner the day he poisoned his business partner. We did a bunch of flowers for Cyril's funeral, which my records say was on February twenty-forth."

"Maldonado died February twenty-second. If he ate ricin-laced food three days before that, it fits in with the time frame the coroner gave me." Max poured himself another cup of coffee. "Got to hand it to you, Darci. That explains the odd plant material found in Cyril's intestines and how it ties in with the ricin poisoning. Like you said, Roy must have taken a handful of those mole bean leaves from his mom's yard during his Sunday visit, cooked 'em until they wilted, and then stirred 'em into the greens in Cyril's plate lunch. That man would eat anything you put in front of him, and I doubt he could've tasted any difference, what with all the bacon drippins they put

162

in the greens over at the diner."

"Or he might've used the beans. I guess he could have soaked his mom's seeds overnight, boiled them, and added those to the pintos. Either way, all his symptoms match what I pulled up on the poison control website." Darci held up the papers she'd printed out earlier, then passed them and the sugar bowl to Max. "His stomach pain, diarrhea, and his organs shutting down. Honestly, it took me a while to figure out the particulars. If Paxton hadn't played around with Wade's tools, I never would've seen that plant in the killer's mom's yard."

"And here I was, feeling sorry for that Nolan bastard. Mae cooked him up a big batch of lasagna and had me take it over to him the day after Cyril died. The son of a bitch."

"Since Roy thinks I'm about to figure out he killed Cyril, I think he tried to shoot me to shut me up before I could tell you." Darci absentmindedly rolled the salt shaker between her palms as one more puzzle piece fell into place. "He must've knocked over the flowerpots, so he'd have a clean shot at me while I picked up the mess."

"No doubt Roy knows we've figured it out for sure now, but he's not stupid enough to sit around waiting for us to go slap cuffs on his wrists. He's most likely on the run, but the good thing to remember is there's no reason for him to hurt you now. I'm sure half the county already knows the law's swarming all over Petal Pushers, and that you've been sitting here, talkin' my ear off all morning." Max squeezed Darci's hand, then

163

dialed one of the deputies.

Darci hoped he was right about Roy not having any reason to use her for target practice again. He was right about word getting around fast, but she hoped Paxton wouldn't hear anything about it until she got a chance to talk to him after school.

"They found shells from a thirty ought six by the tree line, with a perfect view of your side yard. Eddie Miller saw a blue pickup spin gravel when it pulled out of the dirt road, a truck just like Roy's." Max saw how shaken Darci still was, then winked a twinkling blue eye at her. "If you ever get tired of hocking plants, I'll deputize you on the spot.

He stirred more sugar into his coffee. "When we found that insurance policy, we thought it looked suspicious until Mrs. Maldonado told us it was Cyril's idea." The yellow mug, decorated with ladybugs and bumblebee motifs, looked small in his weathered hands. "Living through the war taught him that people could die any minute, and he wanted 'em both to be prepared. When they went into business together, Roy and Cyril each took out a policy with the other as beneficiary, in case one fell off a horse and died, had a heart attack or whatever."

"Why was Roy so desperate for money that he had to kill for it? Everyone said he thought of Cyril as a best friend and a father figure." Darci couldn't imagine killing someone for financial gain, especially someone who'd been as magnanimous as Cyril.

"Roy has a gambling problem, which is no big secret, and he usually loses. Horse races, craps, you name it. I won twenty bucks off him once myself, at one of Nick Hopper's poker parties. Some thugs started asking around, looking for Roy a few months back, and word is he owed six digits."

"Um . . ." Hoyt, a few shades paler than usual, cleared his throat. "You might want to ask Ashley Rosales about that."

"What do you think she knows, son?" Max's notebook was going to be full before the day was over.

"Well, Amber, my girlfriend, is her BFF, so she told her what she overheard in the stable a few weeks after Mr. Maldonado croaked . . . um, died, I mean. Ashley boards over at M & N. She was in the stall grooming her horse, but they didn't see her." Hoyt bit his lip.

"Go on. Who didn't see her?"

"Her boyfriend Jordan told her not to tell anybody, because she might get added to the hit list." Hoyt took a deep breath to steady himself. "Two big Neanderthal looking dudes were all up in Roy's face, smacking him around. Ashley heard him say they'd get their money as soon the insurance paid off. By then, she was hunkered under a horse blanket in the corner of the stall."

"Did she hear anything else?"

"Um, yeah. One of 'em told Roy he'd better be quick with the moolah or his mom's blood would be on his hands too, not just Maldonado's. Said next time they'd do a lot more than just cut her brakes."

"Oh my God." Darci's hand covered her mouth, but didn't stay there long. "I saw Teresa Nolan at Cyril's funeral, sitting next to Roy, with a cast on her arm."

"That's right. She was in a car wreck in January, not long after that big snow we had," Max said. "Guess it was more to it than a slippery road. At least now we know what Roy's motive was. He had to pay off on the gambling debt ASAP, or else they were going to kill his mother. I be damned."

An EMT came into the kitchen carrying a medical bag. It took a second for Darci to figure out he was there to patch up her head. She shot her godfather a look that said calling an ambulance was going just a tad bit overboard.

"Not a word, Darci, just let the man do his job," Max said, knowing full well she'd listen to him. He clicked his ink pen again and turned back to Hoyt. "What's Ashley's address and phone number? Don't worry. I'll talk to her myself, without the squad car, and we'll keep her name out of it, but I have to get a statement."

"Ow!" The medic peeled the Band-aid off her forehead, then dabbed the wound with something that stung like hell and smelled like turpentine.

Darci jumped when the phone rang. Her nerves were a mess, but nothing compared to Wade's. His buddy at the auto parts store down the street called to let him know the cops were hunting for the guy who shot his wife, but that everything should be okay, since the sheriff was down at the flower shop with an ambulance.

Charlotte brought baby Cole by to visit Darci one afternoon near the end of the month. Darci held the baby, kissing his little nose periodically as they sat eating Krispy Kremes at the table.

"Are you sure you can make it a few more weeks without me?" Charlotte asked. "Ashley is all set to babysit, so if you need me to help out before September fifteenth, just say the word. Me and little Cole Thomas are feeling fine, but we're tired of being cooped up in the house, aren't we, baby doll." She reached over to wiggle his teeny foot.

"Be glad you were home safe last week. Did I tell you about the bells?" Darci went on when Charlotte shook her head. "I think the Ghost Lady just might have saved me the other day. Hoyt was in the back and no customers had come in, but when I heard those bells jingle, that's what made me stand up. The second I moved, Roy squeezed off the first shot. If it hadn't been for somebody making that noise, he'd have hit my head instead of that flowerpot."

"I'm just happy you're alright. You wouldn't believe how many people have asked me how you're doing, and for all the details." News in a small town travels lightning fast under normal circumstances, so all the buzz over the county's first murder case since the Civil War sure wasn't a big surprise. Charlotte gave her a big hug, then pushed a highlighted curl away from Darci's forehead. "Think it'll leave a scar?"

"I'm so happy my brains didn't get blown out, I don't even care. Glad I only had to have a butterfly bandage instead of stitches, though."

"Have they caught that asshole yet, or have any leads about where he is?" Charlotte asked.

"They think Roy headed toward Indianapolis. When Max interrogated Belinda Blanford, she spilled her guts on everything she knows about Roy. According to her story, Roy asked her to bring their lunch over the day he poisoned Cyril. He said he stopped by the diner, then had to run back to his house for something and ended up leaving the takeout on his kitchen table."

"And the scuzzy little nitwit didn't find that at all suspicious?" Charlotte rolled her eyes.

"Nope, she even zapped the boxes in the microwave, to make sure the food stayed warm. One carton was dented on the side, which is why she dribbled juice from the greens on herself. Max thinks the dent let Roy know which box was poisoned, but he can't figure out whether he was planning to set Belinda up for the murder by having her bring the stuff over, or if he was so nervous that morning he really did run off and forget it."

"Is she in jail?"

"Max could pretty much tell she didn't know anything about the poisoning, or her boyfriend trying to kill me. The diner receipts show that Roy called February nineteenth for two orders of their special beans, greens, and cornbread, to go.

And the times check out. He let Belinda go but confiscated her cell. Oh, Roy used his credit card to buy gas in northern Indiana. The farther he is from here, the better off I feel."

"What did you tell Paxton about all this? I don't want to goof up and say the wrong thing in front of him."

"After dealing with Wade, Paxton was easy. We told him somebody messed up the Back to School display and used it for target practice, in case any of the kids in his class heard something about the shooting. Know what he said? That the bad guys must've ran away because they were afraid Uncle Max would kick their butts."

"Smart kid," Charlotte said. "Sure I shouldn't come in tomorrow, give you and the ghost a little backup?"

"Don't be silly." Darci couldn't resist smooching the baby once more. "You enjoy your maternity leave. The last thing you need is to overdo it too soon."

"So how's business?" Charlotte washed down a bite of chocolate donut with a glass of milk. She had to avoid coffee for another few weeks, until after she quit breastfeeding.

"Well, since you asked," Darci said, her face darkening, "not the best. We're still getting plenty of customers, that's not the problem."

"Spill it," Charlotte insisted. "What's wrong, Darce?"

"The Smith-Jacobson wedding canceled, after all the out-of-season stuff I special ordered came in." Never one to complain, Darci felt the load on her shoulders lighten just a bit as she spoke. "Their deposit covered part of it, but unless I find somebody just rearing to buy a butt load of Dutch tulips, I don't know how I'm gonna make my money back on them."

"That sucks," Charlotte said. "But knowing you, I bet you'll think of some gimmick to sell at least part of 'em."

"Oh, but it gets worse." Darci consoled herself by nuzzling the baby's cheek against her own. "The stupid transmission went out on the delivery van. After replacing that and putting new tires on the thing, I had to shell out almost five thousand bucks. Money I did *not* have in the budget."

"Here, eat another donut." Charlotte slid the box toward her. "Maybe that'll help.

"Couldn't hurt."

"Okay, that does suck really bad, but it's not the end of the world. You lost money this month, but business is booming, and you're still alive and kickin'. Hey, you're usually Miss Optimistic, so cheer up."

"You're right," Darci said through a mouthful of jelly-filled pastry. "I just need to focus on the positive. Surely we'll come through this just fine. I hope."

Petal Pushers' Plant of the Month for August is

Chrysanthemum
Chrysanthemum spp.
Perennial

Common name: Mums

Brief description: Mums always bring autumn to mind, since they are the most abundant flower of the season. They grow from one to three feet tall and come in colors ranging from pink, red, yellow, purple, orange, and white. Celia Kemp has the prettiest mum display in her front yard, so slow down and take a look if you're driving past her house.

Symbolism: wealth, abundance, a long life, and rest.

Trivia: People who're into Feng Shui think these flowers bring happiness and laughter into your home. The Japanese call the position held by the Emperor the 'Chrysanthemum Throne'.

Growing instructions: They need moist soil in full sun. Pinch garden mums back in early summer to make the plant bushier.

Uses: Plant chrysanthemums in beds, borders, or containers.

Tools & Tips: Everybody needs a good pair of garden shears. Use them to cut back plants, prune rosebushes and shrubs, and cut flowers for arrangements and bouquets. Select a pair with stainless steel blades and handles that feel comfortable in your grip. Take care of this tool by keeping the blades clean and oiling them ever so often, to prevent rust and keep them lubricated. Sharpen when they start to dull. Some people keep a separate pair just for their roses. If you trim off diseased parts, rub down the shears with alcohol to keep from spreading anything to healthy plants.

Chapter Nine

September

Look like the innocent flower,
but be the serpent under 't.
~ William Shakespeare

It was around six o'clock one evening when Wade got a chance to repair the wall. Darci went home to make dinner and left him alone at Petal Pushers with only Daisy the parakeet to keep him company. He took the magazine clipping off the wall and pulled off the tape loops, trying to picture his not so sports minded wife playing an impromptu game of catch in the middle of her flower shop.

"Tell me something, Daisy. What did Darci and Hoyt plan to use for bases?"

The little bird hopped on her swing instead of answering him, and watched as he widened the opening. With his arm shoulder deep inside the wall, he hoped he wouldn't come across any territorial mice while he felt around for the ball.

His fingers brushed against something round. When he tried to grasp it, it rolled farther to the side, still in the wall's interior. Wade reached for it, but closed his fist around something that felt like jagged bits of tile. He pulled out some rather large shards of broken china, and after a few fist-fuls, he pieced them together in the shape of a plate. Black markings on the back of one fragment drew his attention. The design looked like some sort of animal beside a harp in front of a lighthouse.

Familiar with antiques from the restorations he performed on some of the oldest homes in the area, he guessed this piece of china dated from the early to mid-eighteen hundreds. The wall showed signs of a previous repair, so he guessed the dish must've fallen in and broke when the prior damage occurred. The shards held no monetary value, but he couldn't bring himself to toss them in the trashcan. They were pretty, and he was overcome by the notion that Darci might like to see them. Maybe she'd have some idea what to do with them, though he didn't have a clue as to what that might be.

He scooted the pieces to the side and focused on repairing the hole, now that he'd retrieved the missing baseball. He felt around inside the wall thoroughly before he sealed the drywall back up, just to make sure some other long forgotten treasure wasn't hiding there. Stories about odd things-keys, spoons, coins, and old bottles-that fell behind walls of older houses like this one intrigued him and sent his imagination into action. During the Civil War and other lean times, people hid valuables under floorboards and made safe little cubbyholes anywhere that might go undetected. Wade knew that wasn't the case here, but the thought gave him something fun to daydream about as he worked.

With a fresh coat of plaster mud smoothed over the drywall tape, he stood back to admire the job. He'd let it dry for a few hours, then come back to sand the spot and paint the section to match the rest of Petal Pusher's yellow walls. The siding he patched last week could probably use another coat too, when he had the brushes out. Nausea stung the back of his throat as he remembered digging the bullet out of the exterior wall, knowing it was there because Roy Nolan pulled the trigger with Darci in his crosshairs.

Wade put his tools away, then checked the seals around the doors and windows for the umpteenth time. A cold draft had swept over him as he fished out the china pieces, which reminded him of his Honey-Do list. He still couldn't find the source, not very surprising when he realized the temperature was warmer outside than in.

"Huh," he muttered when the notion Darci and Charlotte had about a ghost haunting the shop popped into his head. "That's just ridiculous. Ghost my ass."

The temperature around him dropped so low that for a second, he thought he saw his own breath when he exhaled. Wade jumped back when, for no explainable reason, a book fell from a shelf behind the counter and clattered to the floor. The parakeet chirped and hopped on the bars of her cage the same way she did when Darci stood talking to her.

The hair rose on the back of Wade's neck, then he realized he was holding the hammer-which he didn't even remember reaching for-in the same manner a person preparing to stab someone held a knife, clenched in his fist, cocked back, ready to deliver a blow. What the hell was that weird shadow beside the wall he'd just fixed? He combed his hand through his thick blonde hair, then gathered up his stuff and left as quickly as he could, short of running.

The paint job could wait for a sunny afternoon when he wasn't the only person in the shop. No way in hell did he intend to tell his wife what just happened, not after the ribbing he gave her and Charlotte when they told him Petal Pushers was haunted. Darci's 'I told you so' was not a pleasant thing to hear.

He caught sight of his own nervous smirk reflected in the rearview mirror as he drove home. Still shaking in his work boots, he remembered the girls weren't scared of a ghost whose sole purpose seemed to be curing half-dead plants and sending Daisy into a tweeting frenzy. Well, that and causing the sort of cold spots he'd heard of on documentaries about ghost hunters. He always laughed at those programs, thinking they were one hundred percent pure bullshit. Although he sat behind his steering wheel grinning at the irony of the situation, he didn't think he'd be laughing about ghost stories anytime in the near future.

There was one other very important reason he wouldn't mention the episode to Darci. He sure didn't want to make her worry that Roy was back lurking around, a thought that briefly flitted through Wade's mind when the book fell. What he wouldn't give for a few minutes alone with that son of a bitch. Just himself, Roy, and his solid maple Louisville Slugger.

Lord have mercy, that's the funniest thing I've seen in I don't know how long! I guess I ought to be plum ashamed of myself for scarin' him so bad, especially after he got those pieces out for me, but heaven help us, I couldn't stop myself. The look on his face, the way he grabbed a hold of that hammer, then ran out of here like a scared bunny rabbit. That'll teach him not to poke fun at my girls.

And I know he saw me. I'm gettin' better at that. Only thing is, seems like I have to be around folks quite a few times before it'll work, maybe for us to build up a feel for each other or somethin'. Guess I'll just have to keep poppin' up in front of people til somebody takes the hint.

The first Sunday morning in September, Darci felt nearly as excited as Paxton about the family outing. While Wade drove the three of them to Hopkinsville, their son asked the universal 'are we there yet' question at least a dozen times.

She called Max last night to make sure, again, that there was no chance of Roy Nolan being anywhere in the area. He told her to go on and have a fun day out with Paxton and Wade. Police spotted Roy in Wisconsin and had a team working to track him down.

"Don't worry about a thing," Max had reassured her. "They should have that SOB's ass in a sling before the week's out." She hoped he was right, because she was sick and tired of worrying. Darci took a deep breath and resolved to put the whole mess out of her mind for today.

"Wait, I forgot something." Paxton hopped back in the truck and emerged seconds later with a program the size of a catalog, thick with color photographs and details of the day's events. "I get extra credit if somebody autographs this for me."

"Just remember to be polite when you ask them." Darci didn't know exactly what to expect, this being the first time she'd attended a Pow Wow. A speaker came to Dixon Elementary the previous week and this was the only thing Paxton had talked about since he gave her the flier. Funny thing was, no matter how many times she put it in the drawer, she kept finding the thing on top of her desk when she sat down to work.

Their feet echoed across the short wooden bridge that stretched over a creek into the park. As they waited in line to pay the entrance fee, Paxton rehashed what he knew about the event.

"This is one of the real stops the Cherokees made on their forced march west during eighteen thirty-eight and eighteen thirty-nine, a place where they really camped out. This is so cool! I mean, the Trail of Tears was horrible, but this is a cool way to pay tribute to them. My teacher said it was like the holo . . . hallo . . . . The thing Hitler did to Jewish people during World War Two." His face scrunched as he searched his fourth grade vocabulary for the correct word.

"Holocaust?" Darci suggested.

"Yeah." Paxton looked proud to sound so knowledgeable on a subject. "My teacher said the Indian Removal Act was like a holocaust. Soldiers yanked 'em from their homes and made 'em march on foot for six whole months. Hundreds of Cherokees of all ages died, especially during the cold weather. A couple of chiefs are buried over there." Paxton pointed toward a grove of trees marked by two statues. "There's a museum, too. Can we see it before we leave?"

"Sure, it ought to be interesting." Her excitement grew as they made their way down the walkway into The Trail of Tears Commemorative Park. A drumbeat urged them along, accompanied by a traditional Cherokee song. The scent of incense and fry bread hung in the air.

"Do you hear that, Mom?" Paxton's eyes danced as he took in the sights at the booths they passed. Hand carved wooden statues, authentic buckskin moccasins, books on Native American culture, wooden flutes, and dream catchers and medicine wheels ranging in sizes large enough to decorate a family room wall to tiny keychain versions of each. "They aren't hollerin', that's how they sing."

"You're right, and it sounds pretty cool." Darci fought the urge to smile at his choice of words, but knew the last thing he wanted was for her to think his spiel was cute. Nine-year-old boys hated the word cute, especially when it applied to them.

They found seats near the top of the metal bleachers encircling the area where the singers and emcee were set up. Darci marveled at the men beating drums, raising their voices in unison. It really was a beautiful sound, primitive, yet full of emotion, and brought goose bumps to her arms even in the ninety-degree heat. She was glad trees shaded at least part of the area.

Paxton flipped through his program while he waited for the action to start. "It says performers come from all over the country to compete in the dance contests each year. I bet they win a ton of money."

The first group of dancers were the Tiny Tots, little girls who Darci judged to be seven and under. Wearing gorgeous embroidered dresses with beaded shawls, the little girls twirled and stepped in rhythm to the music. Everyone clapped and cheered when they finished.

A Cherokee storyteller stepped up next, taking the mike from the stand so he could walk around as he spoke. "*Osiyo.* This looks like a sharp crowd, so I guess you all know that means hello in *tsalagi*, or Cherokee." The older gentleman captivated the audience with the slow cadence of his baritone voice as he introduced himself. "I'd like to share a story that I heard as a young child, a story that's been passed down from generation to generation.

"A young boy went walking high up in the mountains on a vision quest, and he came upon a rattlesnake. The boy, warned by his elders never to trust a rattler under any circumstances, was wary of stopping to listen to the snake. But this conniving rattlesnake said, 'Please pick me up and carry me down the mountain. I have been here too long and will surely freeze to death if I don't make it down before nightfall.' The boy's big heart took precedence over his mind that day, so he finally gave in. After the snake promised not to bite him, the boy picked up the rattler and tucked it safely inside his shirt before walking back down the path to the foot of the mountain by a brook. Warmed from being inside the shirt, the snake said, 'Thank you, young man. I'm very grateful for your help. Now can you put me down on a nice warm rock?' The boy reached for the snake inside his shirt. 'Sssssssss', the rattles buzzed. In a flash, the boy felt the sharp fangs sink into his hand. 'Why did you bite me, Mr. Snake? Now I will surely die,' the boy said, hurt that the creature he'd just helped out of the goodness of his heart betrayed him with a poisonous bite. Before slithering away, leaving the boy to lie there suffering as venom coursed through his small body, the snake told him he had no choice. 'I am a rattlesnake, and this is my nature. You knew what I was when you picked me up.'"

Paxton clapped and cheered when the gentle-man finished his story. "*Wado*, thank you", the storyteller said. He waved to the crowd and made his exit.

Darci clapped as well, thinking about the moral. "You *do* get the meaning of his story, don't you Paxton? If something looks like a snake in the grass and you hear it rattling, don't let it smooth talk you into trouble."

"Yeah Mom, I get it." Paxton rolled his eyes.

Teenage girls in the jingle dress competition entered the circle. Three hundred and sixty-five hand-sewn bugle bells jingled on each dress while the dancers twirled and stepped gracefully around the grass. Embroidered shawls draped around their shoulders flared out along extended arms as bells on their ankles tinkled above bead-ed moccasins.

"They're so beautiful," Darci said, alternating her gaze from their dresses to their footwork. "Their toes seem to barely touch the ground."

The emcee called the older boys and men to the tribal circle for the liveliest dance of the day. "Their outfits are way cooler than the girls'," Paxton exclaimed, fascinated by the feathers and bustles on their costumes. In an awe-inspiring display, they twirled sticks with things hanging from the ends as they danced in sweeping whirls, sporadically dropping to a squat and bouncing back up without missing a drumbeat.

"How in the world have I managed to live around here all my life and never found out about the annual Pow Wow until now? We're gonna have to start coming every year." Judging by the wonder spread over Wade and Paxton's faces, Darci wouldn't hear any objections.

The Sheltons sat amazed as act after act held them in their seats. They'd arrived expecting a fun day, but had no idea the quality of entertainment would be this high. During intermission, they tried walking tacos from one of the booths.

"Oh my God, this is delicious," Darci mumbled through her first mouthful. A beef mixture similar to taco meat or chili filled the fry bread base, with cheese and onions heaped on top.

Each carried dessert and a cold drink back to the stands after they scarfed down their lunch. Fry bread was a sweet and tasty delicacy, one Darci decided rivaled even her favorite Krispy Kreme jelly donuts. They'd watched the preparation with watering mouths. The vendor flattened out a ball of dough, then tossed it back and forth between her hands in a movement similar to a chef tossing pizza crusts. When the dough stretched to about the size of a saucer, they tossed it in hot oil to fry, flipping it over when it started to swell. The finished fry bread looked like a cross between puff pastry and a soft fluffy tortilla, topped off with either honey or powdered sugar. Indecisive as usual, Darci waffled between the two, unable to make up her mind. The vendor smiled at her dilemma and let her have both, one on each half, so she could make up her mind which she liked better as she ate.

Back in their seats, the three drank lemon

shakeups and devoured their fry bread while watching the hoop dancer's performance. The yellow fringe on his legs and arms matched the strips dangling from the hoops, which worked their way up and down his body and limbs as if moving of their own volition.

Wade volunteered to get another fry bread for them to split, so long as Darci and Paxton agreed to top it with honey, his personal favorite. Nobody objected, not even his indecisive wife.

By the time Wade came back and sat down, honey dripping onto the extra napkins, the next artist had entered the circle. A Cherokee man, his long dark hair blowing in the gentle breeze, played the flute he'd just told the crowd he made himself, a skill passed down from his grandfather to his father, then on to him. The melody carried a dreamy, surreal quality unlike anything Darci'd ever heard before. The trills from that instrument would make a canary break down in a fit of jealousy. A woozy sensation came over her as she listened, maybe from the combination of her full stomach and the heat; she closed her eyes and the dizzy spell soon passed. As the final notes filled the summer day, the emcee announced that the flutist had a booth set up where the audience could buy his latest CD.

"Sweet!" Paxton bounced up and down on the seat. "*Please*, can I have one? Maybe if I buy one of his CDs, he might give me his autograph."

The flutist had many fans, judging from the cluster of people thronged around his booth waiting for a chance to buy his merchandise and talk to him in person. A lady in line in front of them mentioned that the musician had performed in a few western movies, which left Paxton even more star struck.

Wade spotted fishing lures for sale in a booth to the left as Paxton hugged his autographed program and new CD to his chest.

"Wade, I swear you'd live on a fishing boat if you could figure out how to bring a TV on board and get pizza delivered in the middle of the river." Uninterested in staring at a bunch of tiny hooks and tie lures, Darci told the boys to take their time looking around and to meet her by the lemon shakeup stand in about an hour.

The booths sold a lot of items that caught her eye. She bought a pair of turquoise earrings trimmed in silver; it only took her fifteen minutes to decide between them and a jade necklace, but she was happy with her choice. The next craftsman sold her a hand-beaded bracelet. She snatched up a wooden flute and instruction book, sure Paxton's face would light up when she surprised him with it. As an afterthought, she hoped he wouldn't drive her crazy playing the thing, like with the drums his uncle gave him for Christmas two years ago. Oh well, she still had earplugs tucked in her nightstand, just in case.

Darci noticed an unusual fragrance as she rearranged the bags in her arms. Exotic without the cheap synthetic hint of commercial incense, the scent drew her into the next kiosk. Inside, a Native American women demonstrated something called smudging. A small bundle of sage tied with twine smoldered on a large shell the woman held as she fanned the fragrant smoke with the feather in her other hand. Darci crowded in to hear her speak.

". . . smudging is a popular practice in other cultures, not just with Native American tribes. Smoke from sage and other herbs contains properties for purification and protection. Some people just like the scent, so they lay bundles on the logs in their hearth whenever they light a cozy fire. Others use it instead of incense. Smudging removes negative energy from houses, and it can ward off depression and other physical or mental ailments." Demonstrating on the volunteer, the lady fanned sage smoke toward the man in front of her, telling him to think positive thoughts as smoky wisps swirled around him from toe to head, since she started at the bottom and worked her way up. "This isn't some magical quick fix or miracle cure, but it helps focus positive energy."

Darci remembered an article she read on this subject, in which New Age practitioners, doctors, and scientists discussed the varying aspects of holistic practices, including smudging. The scientists said nothing negative about sage smudges, just that they weren't convinced they did any good. One of the doctors did say she used them to freshen up her office.

This demonstration was every bit as fascinating as the performances going on in the tribal circle. People lined up to buy things afterward, so Darci waited for the crowd to thin out. She picked up a basket and looked through each of the tables lined with goods. Shelves on one wall lined the tent-like structure of the booth, on which neat bundles of sage and other herbs lay in tidy stacks. Baggies safeguarded the finer herb powders like saffron, rather than risk the expensive little pieces blowing away. A table on the far side held a myriad of books, some on Native American culture, medicinal plant use, herbology, and floral crafts. The stand in the center held smudging supplies that included turkey feathers for fanning the smoke and large flat seashells. Darci thought they came from clams until she read the label on the abalone shells. Beside them sat ornately carved wooden boxes made to hold the smudging kits. One of each of those went into her basket, which by this point threatened to overflow. She placed it by the register and picked up a second.

Another table displayed what looked like long two-inch-wide strips constructed of some kind of stiff grass. Darci picked up a bundle, held it to her nose and closed her eyes as she sniffed, pretty sure the intoxicating fragrance from the plaits was responsible for luring her into this little booth of herbal paradise.

Someone beside her laughed, which caused Darci to open her eyes and look around. She felt like a little girl caught sampling the perfume counter at Macy's.

"Smells good, doesn't it?" said the owner of the booth, the woman who'd given the demonstration. "It's called sweetgrass. Here, I'll light a piece of it. I love this stuff, myself. Never get tired of the scent." She introduced herself as Sue, reached under the table for a smaller bundle, and placed it on the abalone shell she'd used for the sage smudge.

"Ahh, this is better than perfume." Darci cupped her hand over the smoldering shell and fanned the smoke toward her nose. "So, do you use this sort of like a room freshener? It smells wonderful."

"I keep some hanging in my house for the scent," Sue explained, "but a lot of people use it in smudges, just like the sage and cedar bundles."

Kids running through the next booth over bumped into a table. Pottery on display shattered to the ground. The unexpected racket drew a startled squeal from Darci's lips as she ducked for cover.

"Sorry." Darci stood back up, embarrassed over making a spectacle of herself. Thankfully, most eyes were turned toward the two people trying to talk their way out of having to pay for what their destructive children just broke. "Guess my nerves got the best of me."

"You don't have anything to worry about." Sue patted Darci's shoulder, then peered deeply into her eyes as if she saw much more than the green flecks in her brown irises. "I get the impression plenty of protective spirits watch over you." She fanned more sweetgrass smoke toward Darci. "Now, what else can I show you?"

When Wade and Paxton grew tired of waiting by the lemon shakeup stand, they found Darci still jabbering away with Sue, piling things on the counter.

Darci loved what she did and loved to shop, she just didn't like spending money. She smiled down at her great deals, eager to set up a new display on Petal Pusher's shelves.

Good thing Wade drove a king cab or all the stuff never would've fit. Paxton carried his new CD and autograph, the flute and music book his mom gave him, some fishing lures he'd picked out, and one of Darci's bags. Wade had a much larger package full of fishing tackle, another with a massive hunting knife in its matching sheath, plus two more of Darci's bags.

"I feel like a human pack horse." Darci shifted her packages, determined not to drop anything. The jewelry she bought rode safely in small cardboard boxes that fit inside her purse, making them the only thing that didn't take up much room. In a sturdy shopping bag, bubble wrap blanketed the carved wooden smudge box she bought for herself. Wade carried her heavier sacks, but she could still see indentations from where those plastic handles had dug into her wrists. The rest of her load consisted of dried herbs, abalone shells, and a few dozen large feathers, the last of which Sue wrapped in tissue paper and placed on top.

Paxton glanced inside the bag he'd been asked to carry, then over at his mother. "Uh, Mom. What's the deal with the tied up sticks in here?" His expression suggested his mom had fallen off her ever-loving rocker.

"Those aren't sticks, silly," Darci said, piling packages and bags behind her seat. "That's sage, sweetgrass, and a few tobacco leaves. I decided to carry some of this holistic stuff in the shop." With everything loaded into the truck, Darci told them about her ideas as they walked toward the museum on the other side of the park.

"What in the world are you going to do with tobacco leaves?" Wade asked, winking under his raised brow. "In case you forgot, we don't smoke."

"I'm gonna familiarize myself with all the traditional uses by reading some of those books you hauled across the parking lot for me," Darci explained. "And people use tobacco to keep bugs out of places. Grandma Odette packed a few leaves in with her wedding dress. She told us kids it kept the moths away. Seemed to work. Anyway, I thought I'd put some in the new display, in case anybody comes asking for an all-natural insect repellant."

"Sounds like this new line should be pretty interesting. Good idea, Hon." Wade took her hand in his as they walked. "What do ya want to bet you'll get a few teenage potheads trying to smoke some of that sage in a water bong. That'd be pretty funny, huh?" They laughed until Paxton interrupted with a question.

"What's a water bomb and why would you put a bunch of dead weeds in one?" The grownups tried to straighten their faces but failed miserably. "Is it like a water balloon? Could me and Hoyt test 'em out for you?"

"Don't think that'd be such a hot idea, son,"

Wade said, wiping the laughter from his eyes, then he cracked up again at the thought.

"I think you misunderstood your dad, because he was just talking nonsense." Darci elbowed Wade in the stomach, then shot him one of her 'look what you've gone and done now' smirks. "We better go in the Heritage Center before it gets crowded."

A guide led the way through the tiny museum inside an authentic log cabin. Glass display cases brimming with authentic memorabilia and artifacts from the Trail of Tears lined the hand-hewn log walls. Pictures of Cherokee Chief John Ross and his family made the whole Pow Wow experience even more personal, putting real faces to the horror of the march.

There were other sights to see on that side of the park after they left the museum. Statues of Chief Whitepath and Fly Smith, two Cherokee chiefs who died on the trail, stood near a small grove of trees. Their graves and a few others rested on the hill behind it, adorned with a small stones, quarters, and shredded tobacco emptied from unsmoked cigarettes people passing through had left to show their respect.

"How about a picture of you two standing in front of the monument?" Darci whipped out her camera while Wade and Paxton struck poses in front of the statues.

Conversation on the ride home shifted between Paxton's ideas for his history project on the Trail of Tears and Wade's eagerness to try out his new fishing tackle. Darci daydreamed about the display she would arrange with her new loot, which she hoped would make up for the money she lost last month on those stupid Dutch tulips.

"Good afternoon." Darci thought she recognized the well-dressed gentleman even though the back of his head was the only thing she could see at the moment, since he'd stopped to look at a cluster of cut glass vases and candle holders. "What can I help you with today?"

"Wade asked me to stop by, to pick up some paperwork he left for me." He spun around, stepped forward, and flashed a politician's unmistakable smile. If baby Cole was here, she knew this guy's lips would be all over him, just like they'd be all over every voter's backside when election time rolled around next year. He extended his hand. "I'm Stetson Clydell, and you must be Darci."

"Sure am, and I've got your stuff right here." She shook his hand, then slid a manila envelope across the counter.

The room temperature dropped dramatically as an uneasy feeling overcame her. She had no idea why, but she wanted this man to leave. Wade worked all weekend on estimates and such, hoping to get the bid for the very lucrative additions to Clydell Manor, one of the nicest historic homes in Webster County. Fighting her unexplained desire to tell the man to take his crap and get out of her shop, she forced herself to be polite.

"Wade's looking forward to working on this project, if everything works out. He was disappointed that he couldn't be here to talk to you himself, but he had some emergency repairs to do on a client's home in Slaughters that was damaged in that storm. A tree came down and took a chunk out of the roof, but at least everybody's okay."

"That's fine. It'll be spring before we get started on it, but that should give my wife and I plenty of time agree on the particulars." A mask of practiced concern replaced his politician's grin as he brushed fingers through his dark wavy hair, surprising Darci when he didn't catch his pinky ring on any wayward curls. "Please do pass on my sympathy to that homeowner. Emergency aid is high on my list of priorities. Shelters, first responders, everything in the system will get updated as soon as I take office."

Damn, she hoped this dipstick wouldn't launch into one of his campaign speeches. One politician was about as bad as the next, in her humble opinion, and she frankly didn't give two hoots in hell who won the next race for Kentucky State Representative. The Clydells had been in one office or another for at least four generations, so she figured he had a pretty good chance at winning, not that she gave a crap.

She still didn't understand why this man was on her last nerve. He was harmless, she wasn't in any danger, and his behavior wasn't anything that should have brought up her radar. The fact that Roy Nolan hadn't been arrested yet probably just made her more nervous than she ought to be.

Right as Stetson picked up the envelope with Wade's estimate inside, the front door blew open. Considering that there hadn't been any hint of a breeze this hot and balmy afternoon, along with the cold spot that hovered in the room, Darci felt pretty sure the Ghost Lady was responsible.

"Ouch!" Stetson shifted the envelope to his other hand and held his right fingertips up in front of his eyes. He glanced back at the manila edges, confused. "Now how did I manage to get a paper cut across three of my fingers? Guess the door banging against the wall must've startled me."

"Latch probably didn't catch when you came in." She wondered what had drawn the Ghost Lady's attention, and why she picked now to learn how to turn a door knob. Darci's unease had doubled in the last few seconds, and she had absolutely no inclination to offer Stetson a Band-Aid or anything else.

"Yeah, that's part of the joy in having one of these older houses. Mine's the same way. The more it settles, the more it creaks. Had to have the bottom of the pantry door planed off nearly two inches last year, when the settling had it dragging the floor. See, I believe your husband will have plenty to keep him busy over at our place." His wink made her skin crawl. She tried not to flinch, since Wade had his heart set on the job at Clydell Manor. "Have him give me a call sometime next week."

The gust of wind that blew the door open acted with the same force in closing it behind Stetson Clydell. The slam rang through Petal Pushers.

You better go, Clydell! And don't you ever show your face back here again.

So many memories ticklin' around in my head, but they just cloud over before I can see 'em real clear. I cain't recollect how certain things came to be, but one thing I do know is that whole blessed Clydell clan ain't nothing but trouble, and down-right dangerous. My head felt like it was about to split right in two when he walked through that door, and a rage I haven't felt in years boiled up inside me. I won't have him hurtin' Darci like he's hurt other folks. That man doesn't have no business comin' around here.

Petal Pushers Plant of the Month for September is

Sweetgrass
Hierochloe odorata
(Not to be confused with *Muhlenbergia filipes*)
Perennial

Common name: Buffalo Grass, Seneca Grass, Bluejoint, or Vanilla Grass.

Brief description: Sweetgrass is native to North America and Europe. The dark green leaves grow to about two feet tall. The aroma is absolutely intoxicating, and I can't make myself or my customers quit sniffing it.

Symbolism: peace and healing.

Trivia: This sacred plant of Native Americans is used for smudging. Sweetgrass is also used in basket weaving.

Growing instructions: Grow in full sun or partial shade and keep the soil moist. Sweetgrass blooms from June to August.

Uses: The grass should be cut, braided, and

dried in late June or early July.

Tools & Tips: Ants driving you bonkers crawling all over your plants and veggies? Cancel that order for the anteater and start saving up your used coffee grounds instead. Sprinkle them in a solid line around the base of your plants, and the little pests will stay away. They don't like to crawl over the coffee grounds. Cappuccino anyone?

Chapter Ten

October

Flowers have spoken to me more than I can tell in written words. They are the hieroglyphics of angels, loved by all men for the beauty of their character, though few can decipher even fragments of their meaning.
~ Lydia M. Child

"Hey, Mom!" Paxton opened and closed the fridge in Petal Pushers' kitchen but ignored the healthy stuff his mom kept there. He rummaged through the cabinets for junk food. "Sweet." The bag of chocolate covered pretzels would do the trick.

"What's up?" Darci trotted down the steps and into the kitchen. She tousled his wavy hair as he poured himself a glass of chocolate milk. "I was straightening up when I heard you holler for me."

"I wasn't sure if you knew there's a customer out front." That was all the conversation he could manage before he dug into his afterschool snack.

"Huh, that's funny. I didn't even hear the bells on the front door jingle." Darci set a napkin in front of Paxton and hurried to the front of the shop.

She returned a couple minutes later, pulled out a chair, and took a seat beside Paxton, commandeering a couple of his chocolate pretzels.

"They must have left. Who was it?" She popped a piece in her mouth. She would never understand why some people took up heroin and cocaine when chocolate and pastry were just as addictive.

"Don't know." Paxton shrugged. "Just some old lady."

"Coming from you, she could be anywhere between twenty-five and two hundred. What'd she look like?"

"Well," he began, scrunching his forehead as he chewed, "she was old. I guess about the same age as you and Charlotte, or Grandma."

In times like this, Darci sympathized with Homer Simpson's habit of choking the living daylights out of Bart.

"She had on a long dark dress, and her hair was stuck up on top of her head like the Mennonite ladies we buy fudge and sweet potatoes from." Paxton took a swig of milk, then wiped his mouth on the back of his hand rather than this napkin. "But her clothes weren't like that, 'cause she had a pin thing on the front of her dress, and I know Mennonites aren't allowed to wear jewelry."

Darci struggled to swallow the bite in her

mouth, which had suddenly gone dry. The clothes and old-fashioned hairdo were one thing, but the broach was the real clincher. She took a gulp from Paxton's glass, then hid her expression behind a napkin until she composed herself. No one mentioned the Ghost Lady in front of the nine-year-old, afraid of scaring the holy crap out of him. His imagination ran full throttle most of the time and she didn't want him to think boogeymen waited around each corner.

"You're right, the Mennonites don't wear any jewelry." Paxton beamed at her acknowledgement, his smile doing much more to calm Darci's nerves than the milk had. "So what was this lady doing? Looking at the display table or the houseplants?"

"Nope, she was beside Daisy's cage when I came in, then she went over toward the porthole and stopped. It was kinda weird. She turned to the wall and rubbed it with her hand." Paxton shook his head and grabbed another pretzel.

"That does sound sort of peculiar." Darci thought for a minute. "Did she say anything to you?"

"Nope."

"And did you say anything to her, or just stand there gawking?" Darci asked.

"Mom," Paxton drawled out in three exasperated syllables that bordered on a whine, but not quite. His mother did not allow whining. He rolled his eyes, which he usually got away with. "She didn't talk to me so I didn't bother her by talkin' to her, either. I don't even think she noticed I was there, 'cause she didn't look at me or anything."

"Now I know you were raised to have better manners than that." Darci couldn't believe she was giving her son a lecture over the politically correct way to treat a ghost. She just couldn't excuse rudeness, poltergeist or not. "You really should have said hello to the lady before you scampered in here to eat. Think you can remember that next time?"

Paxton sighed, then responded, a singsong lilt in his voice. "Yes ma'am. I should say hello or something to people I don't even know to be polite before I have a snack."

"Well, yeah." Darci smirked, knowing she'd used the same tone on her own mother as a child. "The shop is kind of like an extension of our home, and if you walk in our house or in here and see anybody, just please say hello next time. Hmmm?"

"Okay, I get it," he said. "Can I go outside now?"

"Sure, Pax, as soon as you clean up your snack mess."

When the back door shut behind Paxton, Darci went to stand by Daisy's cage. The parakeet hopped on the bars beside the door, bobbling her head, expecting Darci to let her out. Unable to resist, Darci pulled the door open and extended her index finger. "Step up." The little bird hopped on, then ran up Darci's arm and perched on her shoulder.

Darci took a few steps toward the round porthole window, trying to retrace the Ghost Lady's steps. She stopped and turned toward the wall to look for anything unusual. An empty sunflower yellow wall stared back at her. What would attract a ghost's attention? Daisy chirped as Darci reached out to touch the smooth plaster the way Paxton's 'old lady' had earlier. She found nothing out of the ordinary.

She wasn't afraid of who or whatever caused these inexplicable episodes, she just found them unnerving. Even Wade couldn't find a logical reason for the cold spots, especially when the air conditioning was off and it was ninety-eight degrees outside. Three people-herself, Charlotte, and now Paxton-couldn't possibly imagine seeing the same figure in a dark outfit from another century, with the same shiny broach pinned to her chest. This wasn't likely to be a prank, not when a pregnant woman worked here; everybody in town knew Jimbo would stomp their asses for even thinking about bothering Charlotte, now and before baby Cole was born. And there was the matter of nearly dead plants miraculously turning into the picture of health overnight, thanks apparently to a ghostly green thumb. No way could any stretch of the imagination explain that.

Her curiosity piqued, Darci found it difficult to concentrate on much else the rest of the day. Luckily, her job didn't involve sharp objects, heavy equipment, or mathematical equations, all of which she would have done damage with in her distracted state. While she put together some autumn wreaths, her thoughts continually drifted back to the image of the Ghost Lady. Who was she and what sort of unfinished business made her appear in the shop? The climax of good horror shows always revealed what wrong needed righting or who needed to be avenged so the spirit could finally cross to the other side, go into the light, or whatever it took to get them to stop haunting people.

Before locking up for the night, she dipped into her filing cabinet and took out the folder labeled 'Deed'. A quick perusal showed Walter H. Brown and his wife Adelaide as original owners of the building that was now Petal Pushers. They deeded the home over to their son William in 1911, and the house stayed in the Brown family until Darci bought it.

She swung by the library on her way home, hoping to find information about the people who used to live in her flower shop. The library stayed open until seven that night, so by the time she drove across town and got Paxton situated in the kid's section, she had a little over an hour. Mrs. Greeley, the librarian, lent a hand, seizing a large book from the genealogy shelf to find cemetery information on the Browns. It listed Walter H. and Adelaide Brown buried in Sweet Grove Cemetery in Lisman, Kentucky. The birth and death dates inscribed on the tombstone were in the book. Born in 1857, Walter died in 1912 while Addie lived from 1864 until 1941.

Darci jotted down the dates while Mrs. Greeley retrieved another volume from the genealogy section, this one devoted to the Brown family history. The index pointed them to a couple pages that gave Walter and Addie's date of marriage as 1879 and information about their three kids. The librarian made copies of those while Darci looked through microfilm for obituaries or articles with information on the former occupants.

Her main objective for this research was to find out who, if anyone, had died in the house, since that would probably be who was doing the haunting. She hoped she wouldn't discover any murders or violent crimes committed on her property, even though it would have occurred before she was born. From the cemetery records, she knew three Brown children had lived to raise families of their own. While that didn't rule them out, it made them less likely. As far as she could tell, those five people had been the only ones to live in the house.

Time was running short. When Darci found Addie's obit, she pushed a button on the machine and watched it spit out a copy from the local newspaper's microfilm. She couldn't find one for Walter's 1912 death. Mrs. Greeley said that wasn't unusual, since people didn't always have death announcements back then. Darci accidentally hit the wrong button when she was finished, then punched rewind and stop. It had been a few years since she'd used one of these things, after all.

When the film jarred to a stop, a headline caught her attention. 'Chamber of Commerce Names Walt Brown Businessman of the Year'. She skimmed the first few lines before she noticed the picture to the right that went with the article. She glossed over the name of the presenter, not giving two hoots in hell who he was, then read Walt and Addie's names in the caption. She stabbed the print button, her eyes fluttering back to the picture while the old machine buzzed and hummed.

Dressed in a coat and hat, Walter was a tall man with a warm smile barely visible under his bushy mustache. Adelaide stood beside him wearing a long skirt and white blouse with dozens of buttons down the front. Kindness emanated from her face, even in the old black and white picture. Though she couldn't tell what color Addie's eyes were, they danced above her smile. A large hat balanced atop her hairdo, no doubt secured with one of those horrendous hatpins like her great-grandmother used to display on the dresser.

Closing time forced Darci to put away the microfilm and turn off the machine. She stacked her printouts with the Man of the Year article on top. As she straightened the stack, her eyes locked on something she hadn't noticed before. She'd been trying to tell if the woman in the photo looked like the one she'd seen in her shop, but she just wasn't sure. Now, with her eyes glued on Addie Brown's silky blouse, there wasn't a doubt in her mind. The unmistakable broach pinned to the left of her placket proved she and the Ghost Lady were one and the same.

"Are you alright, Ma'am?" Mrs. Greeley asked. "You're so pale, and you look startled."

"No, I'm fine, thanks." Darci pulled herself together Scarlett O'Hara style, silently vowing to
think about it later. "I just swallowed my gum,"
she said, the only logical reason she could think
of to explain her expression. She had no intention of telling the nice librarian that she'd just
found a picture of the dead woman whose ghost
haunted her flower store, miraculously healed
dead plants, helped her dodge a bullet to the
head, entertained her parakeet, and kept down
the cooling bill with bursts of cold air. She hated
to lie, but this little white one kept her from
sounding like the biggest Brazil nut in the fruit-
cake.

After supper that night, Darci took a nice hot
bubble bath and slipped into her nightgown,
chenille housecoat, and cushy slippers before
treading back downstairs to read through the
stack of information she'd copied. She'd tried to
keep her mind off the photo while she ate, but
kept catching herself staring at the papers piled
on the side table. Three times she'd opened her
mouth to tell Wade what she found, then stuffed
food in it instead when she remembered how he'd
made fun of her for believing in ghosts. No, she
thought it best to wait until she read over the articles and had a chance to mull things over before telling him about it. Wade sat in the next
room watching some kind of sports crap on television, something sure to keep him too busy to

catch her poring over the papers.

Darci put the stack on the dining room table and went to the kitchen to make a cup of coffee. She put the filter in the coffeemaker, then stopped. She might need something a bit stronger to settle her nerves. The Ghost Lady didn't scare her, but until this afternoon she'd sort of expected some logical explanation to turn up. Undisputable evidence of an otherworldly being that existed in Petal Pushers proved a tad bit unsettling.

She lifted a wine glass from the rack above the kitchen sink and placed it beside the coffeepot. Booze or caffeine, how would she ever decide? In spite her supper an hour before, stress made her stomach rumble for something sugary. Wade had brought home a dozen assorted Krispy Kremes, so she put two on a plate. At least that was an easy decision. Coffee went with donuts, but she hankered for the calming effect of red wine. Her eyes darted from donuts to coffee to the wine glass, then fell on the liquor cabinet.

She returned to the dining room carrying the plate of donuts and Kahlua-laced coffee.

Determined to take her time on each document, she started with the obituary. It should provide the most information, plus she hoped to get more Kahlua in her system before she caught another glimpse of the photograph. She read Adelaide 'Addie' Brown's death announcement straight through, paused to wash down a bite of cruller with a sip of coffee, then reread it more carefully.

"Aha, I knew it! She died in the shop." The obit said Addie died in her home, the same building that now housed Petal Pushers, from injuries due to a falling accident. "No mention of suspicious circumstances or an investigation, just a fatal fall, a common accident for elderly people. Thank God she wasn't murdered. No telling what I'd have running around behind the counter if that were the case."

"What Hon? You say something?" Wade called from the living room.

"No, I'm just reading," she answered. A second later she heard him cheering at the game, her babble forgotten. Darci yelled back at theater screens, so it made perfect sense that she would talk back to the books she read. Especially novels by Stephen King or Dean Koontz. She only hoped things wouldn't get as eerie as one of their plots. So far, the Ghost Lady seemed no worse than Casper with a green thumb and she sincerely hoped it stayed that way.

Back to the obit. Addie died at the ripe old age of seventy-seven, preceded in death by Walter nearly thirty years before. It listed her three children along with their state and city of residence. All had moved away; William lived in Tennessee, Virginia moved to Indiana with her husband, and George lived two hours away in Louisville. The article ended with 'Mrs. Brown was a member of the First Baptist church, active in the Botanical Society of Webster County, and aided many women of this fine county by acting as midwife.'

"So Addie was in a botanical group." Darci

guessed that's where she learned to work miracles on plants. The midwife thing struck her as pretty neat, too. She never really gave it much thought before, but knew her grandparents were born in their homes instead of hospitals. She guessed it made sense that midwives would deliver as many babies as doctors in small rural areas, especially during that time period.

The next few pages were copies from the Brown family genealogy, the librarian having Xeroxed everything pertaining to Walter and Addie. Walter, the third generation of his family born in Virginia, migrated to Kentucky as a small boy when his parents received a land grant. Adelaide McGee's parents came from Ireland, then settled in North Carolina for a couple years before they moved on to Kentucky, where Addie was born. Both Walter and Addie had long lists of brothers and sisters, another thing common for a time when so many children died during infancy and those who survived helped on the family farm.

The genealogy went back five generations on Walter's side, but dealt primarily with the Browns rather than Addie's McGee line. Darci thought it best to focus more on Addie's ancestors and descendants, since it was her spirit that haunted Petal Pushers. The genealogy listed birth, death, and marriage dates for Walt and Addie's three children, their spouses' names, and grandchildren born before the genealogy's compilation in 1952. She highlighted those names with a green marker.

At last she came to the 'Man of the Year' head-line and Addie's picture. Darci took a bathroom break, refilled her coffee and Kahlua, and then went to work nibbling her second Krispy Kreme as she studied the article. She covered the photo-graph with a notepad as she chewed, to put off looking at it a little longer.

The piece talked mainly about Walt Brown and his achievements at the county's first insurance agency, the business that won him the Chamber of Commerce's award for businessman of the year. At least when Addie became a widow, Walt's profession meant he undoubtedly left her benefi-ciary to a sizeable life insurance policy. Widow-hood was Darci's greatest fear, and she was relieved to know Adelaide Brown had been well provided for after her husband's death.

The section about Walt's personal life called Addie a devoted wife and mother. That paragraph also named their only child at that time, Willie, and the family dog, which kind of shows the im-portance of women and children in the later part of the nineteenth century. When the reporter de-scribed the Brown's home, he mentioned a stun-ning garden that encompassed most of the yard. Attributing it to Mrs. Brown's interests in botani-cals, he said it rivaled the beauty of those he'd seen when traveling in England, which had in-cluded tours of the palace grounds.

Darci soaked in the information. "Wow." Addie loved botany. The devotion it would have taken to fill the lawn with well-maintained plants during her lifetime, before the invention of gas powered lawnmowers and Miracle Gro, was really amazing.

"You say something, Hon," Wade called again, still perched in front of the television. "Or are you still reading?"

"Still reading, Babe. Don't let me distract you from the game." Darci rolled her eyes, but grinned.

"Okay. Enjoy your book." Three seconds passed before Darci heard him jump off the couch. "Oh, yeah, that's the way to do it!" Apparently, his team scored a basket, touchdown, homerun, or whatever the hell they did to make points. Darci never understood the male infatuation with watching grown men chase balls all over the place.

She moved the notepad off the black and white photograph and drained the last drop of caffeinated Kahlua, then scrutinized Addie's face. Coincidences became apparent. Both mothers spent their lives in Webster County, and she and Addie shared an obsession with plants and flowers. Darci worked in the same building Addie and Walt called home. Staring at the photograph, she noticed they both had dark hair, though that seemed to be the only physical resemblance. Their builds were quite different, Addie being slender and petite while Darci, well, she enjoyed good food more than fitting into tiny clothes.

The Brown heirs put the house on the market at the exact time Darci got a business loan, which had to be the oddest fluke of all. After planning for the delivery van and massive startup cost involved in purchasing all the floral equip-ment, supplies, and plants, the house came in a few thousand under budget. Darci signed the closing agreement within twenty-four hours of finding it, something which made her realtor very happy.

She carried her empty plate to the kitchen and set it in the sink. Coffee cup in hand, she didn't need any more caffeine this close to bedtime, opt-ing instead for straight Kahlua over ice. She usu-ally consumed one or two glasses of wine a week, but with what she'd uncovered about Miss Addie, she thought the three drinks spaced over two hours this evening were well justified. With her kid asleep in bed and ESPN doing a fine job of keeping her husband entertained, it wasn't like she was slacking on her responsibilities. Plus, poor Wade wouldn't get any sleep if she sat awake all night in bed jabbering about Addie. Nope, these late night cocktails were definitely a good idea.

With the sheets of paper spread in front of her, she realized destiny helped her buy the old Brown homestead. There just wasn't any getting around that. Addie would have appreciated the fact that Petal Pushers sold beautiful plants and stocked exotic flowers all year round. Some of the blossoms she used in arrangements were hybrids that hadn't even existed when Addie was alive, specimens guaranteed to strike the botanist's fancy if they caught her eye during her ghostly strolls through the shop. Darci wondered if Addie could see things as they were now, in the present day, or whether the ghost only saw things as they'd been nearly a hundred years ago.

The answer became clear and she took another nip. Addie had to see everything in the here and now to heal those sick plants. Plus, people noticed her looking directly at Daisy, and the parakeet certainly responded to her attention with a symphony of tweets.

Adelaide Brown had been a midwife. Could that be the reason why Charlotte was the first to see the Ghost Lady, and saw her more frequently than anybody else had?

That still left the big question. Why was Addie haunting the shop? Did her presence mean she needed to attend to some unfinished business? Or could it be that her love of plants and home drew her back of her own choosing?

"Oh hell. I don't know whether to buy a Ouija board or call an exorcist."

The booze overpowered the caffeine. Drowsy, she put the papers away and called it a night. Snuggled under her covers, she chose to look on the bright side. If Petal Pushers had to be haunted, Addie Brown was the best choice for the job. The face photographed for the newspaper so long ago belonged to a happy and loving person, one who didn't scare Darci in the least.

The New Age display drew a wider range of people into Petal Pushers, some a little kooky, but harmless. Darci straightened up the smudging supplies she bought from Sue, the sage bundles, the sweetgrass she couldn't make herself or her customers stop sniffing, and the abalone shells. She rearranged herbal books to fill the gap left by the missing tobacco leaves.

An elderly lady came in the day before asking about them. "My husband used to raise tobacco, but his last crop was several years ago. I've been missing the extra leaves we used to keep pesky ole bugs away from our off-season clothes and whatnot." She leaned in to whisper, "Moths can do a number on your unmentionables, you know." She bought the whole supply.

"How's my favorite florist doin' is afternoon?"

"Always better when you stop by." Darci turned in Max's direction. She was glad to see him, but he hardly ever made a visit while on duty. The last time that happened, she'd just been shot at. That made her wonder why he was here, and hope it wasn't bad news. "How's your day going?"

"One of the best I've had in a while," Max said, his grin letting her know everything was fine. "I just got word that Roy Nolan's been arrested. The Ohio State Police caught him hidin' out at his cousin's place in Cincinnati. They dug the snivelin' bastard out of a pile of laundry in the bathroom closet."

"Thank God." Darci caught Max in a bear hug. "Maybe now I can quit jumping out of my skin at every little sound."

"No reason to ever worry about that little piss ant again. Came out from under the pile of dirty underwear bawling like a baby, begging not to be locked up. He confessed to everything, poisoning Cyril, and what he tried to do to you. They'll transport his ass back here in a few days, where he'll stay in a cozy little cell I'll personally watch over until his trial. Then I guess he'll spend the rest of his sorry life in the state pen," Max said. "Roy would've got away with murder if that mole bean plant hadn't caught your eye."

"I about got my stupid self killed, though. Now I know it's not such a hot idea for me to go collecting evidence from a killer's mama's house, should it ever come up again in the future." Darci sighed. "And I hope it never does."

Petal Pushers' Plant of the Month for October is

Boston Fern
Nephrolepis exaltata
Perennial

Common name: Sword Fern

Brief description: This has been a favorite houseplant since Victorian times. The Boston fern, with its delicate fronds, can reach up to five feet in diameter.

Symbolism: magic, discretion, and shelter.

Trivia: Boston ferns are great at absorbing formaldehyde and other toxins from the air.

Growing instructions: Boston ferns like high humidity and medium light, never full direct sun. Temperatures between sixty and seventy-five degrees are ideal for these houseplants. Remove brown fronds, both to cut back on having to vacuum around them up and to encourage new growth. Mist your ferns daily.

There are two schools of thought on how to water these babies. Donovan Lewis says to water them often and keep the soil damp to the touch. Blanche Blanford swears by letting her ferns soak up water in the sink for a few hours, and then not water them again until the dirt is dry to the touch.

Uses: These are perfect in hanging baskets or set on pedestals out of direct sun.

Tools & Tips: Get double duty and a big bang for your buck with the pumpkins you'll see for sale from now to the end of the year. First, use them for decorations on the porch or around your yard, or even inside for centerpieces or by the hearth. Second, after you're sick of looking at them, bake them up and use them in your favorite seasonal or holiday recipes. They taste so much better than the crap out of a can, are easy to prepare, and can be frozen for the months to come.

How to Roast a Pumpkin

This also works for other winter squash, just vary the cooking time according to the size you use.

1. Clean the outside of the pumpkin, cut it in half, and take out the pumpkin guts. (You might want to save the seeds to feed the birds and squirrels, or make a snack out of them by baking and tossing them with sugar or spices.)

2. Place the pumpkin halves cut side down in a baking pan or roaster and cover with a lid or aluminum foil.

3. Bake at 450 degrees for about forty-five minutes to an hour, or until the flesh is easily pierced with a fork.

4. After it cools, scoop out the pumpkin and puree it or mash it with a potato masher.

5. Cook with it now or store it in the freezer. Use just like you would plain canned pumpkin, in soup, pie, cake, cookies, or casseroles.

Chapter Eleven

November

A profusion of pink roses
bending ragged in the rain
speaks to me of all gentleness and its enduring.
~ William Carlos Williams

Jingling bells on the front door alerted Darci that she had customers. That sound meant she needed to drop what she was doing, engage in a little small talk, and try to make a sale. She'd met so many interesting people, it was fine with her when folks just wanted to come in to get a feel for the shop, or to spread the latest gossip.

"Good morning," Darci greeted an older couple she'd never seen before. "What can I help you with today?"

The woman stood in the center of the room, one hand clasped over her chest as she took in every detail around her. Approval and wonder radiated across her face.

"You'll have to excuse my wife." The gentleman handed a handkerchief to his spouse, to wipe the tear that slid down her cheek. "Hattie's grandparents used to live here, so she's a bit nostalgic."

Hattie dabbed at her eyes and blew her nose. "I'm just being silly." She folded the hankie and gave it back to him. The gentleman seemed to think she'd need it again, so he palmed it in his hand rather than return it to his pocket. "I haven't been here since I was a little girl, when Grandma was still alive."

I swany, I cain't believe it! It's my Hattie girl! She's grown so old. Last time I saw her, she was still little enough to sit in my lap. She still has those same pretty eyes, but with my grandmother's wrinkles on her sweet face.

Where did the years go? I cain't remember a thing about her growin' up, gettin' married to this fella, nothin' after little Hattie's sixth birthday.

"Oh, so the Browns were your grandparents? It's so nice to have you stop by. Do y'all live around here?"

This is amazing, Darci thought. Just a few days ago, she'd read through the Brown family history, and today one of Addie and Walt's descendants walked right through the front door.

"No, we're from Tennessee, around Clarksville. We were visiting some relatives up in Mount Vernon and I just had a hankering to stop by and see if Grandma's place was still standing. Wanted to show it to Gene, here." She motioned toward her husband.

"Please, feel free to look around anywhere you like." Darci couldn't believe she was talking to Addie and Walter's granddaughter. So many questions ran through her mind, she didn't know where to start.

"My Uncle George lived here for a little while after his wife died, but he moved on back to Louisville before we had a chance to drop by. He had some work done to the place, it'd been empty so long then. Seems like he said there was water damage from the roof leakin' and he had to patch up the bedroom floor and the drywall in the parlor. Sure can't tell it now, though. You've got this house shined up like a new penny."

Hattie led the way, explaining how each room looked when she'd last been in the house. She pointed out where her grandparents' four-poster bed used to stand in their second floor bedroom, the place of honor the grandfather clock once occupied on the staircase landing, and where the old coal stove sat in the kitchen. Captivated by every word, Darci imagined Petal Pushers as a museum and herself getting the grand tour. Hattie's vivid descriptions made it easy to visualize things as they had been a lifetime ago.

"We used to love playing down in the root cellar. It stayed so cool on hot summer days. Don't think I can face going back down there now, though. Not after . . . ." Hattie turned pale, covered her mouth with hand for a minute, and shook her head. "You probably don't know this, but they found Grandma down there. Said she must've fell carrying jars of strawberry preserves she'd made. Aunt Virginia said she didn't understand what got into her, why she didn't wait until the following week, like they planned. She was supposed to bring her girls down then, so they could help her with the canning and such." She forced a grin and tried to shake off the sad memory. "Grandma always was a little stubborn, though, once she got an idea in her head."

"I'm so sorry." Miss Addie's obituary mentioned death by falling, but Darci had no idea where the accident had taken place. She used the space for extra storage and like most old cellars, it was dark, creepy, and full of spider webs. Now it seemed weird that nothing out of the ordinary happened when she and Hoyt took stuff down there, since that's where the ghost had died. Then again, she did usually get a gloomy sort of feeling at the bottom of those steps, and a cold spot wouldn't be as obvious in a room that stayed cooler than the temperature outdoors.

"I was young when Grandma died, so it's a real blessing to be able to remember the things about her I do," Hattie explained. "What isn't from my own memory comes from pictures I've seen in the family album and the stories my daddy told as I grew up. And I used to spend a few weeks here with Grandma each summer before she passed away." A faraway look sparkled in her eyes.

Died!! Passed away?! I don't know what in tar-nation you're goin' on about, but your grandmam-my is most certainly not dead! What in the world's wrong with you? Somebody must be a pullin' your leg about that other stuff too, 'cause I've got better sense than to go and fall down my own cellar stairs. You know I always hang on to that banister and take it one step at a time.

I swany, you better not let me find out you've been hittin' the hootch this early in the day, little miss, grown married woman or not.

"What was Addie like?" Darci rested her chin in her hands with her elbows propped on the counter. She wanted to hear every detail.

"Oh, she was just the sweetest person you'd ever want to meet," Hattie began. "Daddy always said there wasn't a person in the whole county who didn't love Addie Brown. As a midwife, she delivered most of the people who lived around here. Grandma was so full of life, even when she got old. She loved babies, kids, and animals. The summer I turned five, she bought me a little pygmy goat that wasn't much bigger than a pup-py. Kept him tied in the corner of the backyard until that fall, when he learned how to chew through the rope to get at Grandma's flowers. Oh, was she miffed! Well, she fussed a little, but mainly I think she liked telling the story. She gave him to some kids out in the country and we got a kitten on my next visit. Grandma figured cats wouldn't mess up her garden. Did I tell you

225

about her garden, yet? I've been gabbing so much it's hard to remember. Hope I'm not boring you."

"Oh, for goodness sake, no! Listening to you is like having history come to life. I'd love to hear about Miss Addie's garden." Darci meant it. Her grin widened when she realized she'd used 'Miss' in front of Addie's name. With all the new information about their resident ghost, she felt as if she knew her.

"You know, that's what everybody called her, except us kids, of course. Miss Addie." Hattie smiled, possibly recalling countless conversations she'd overheard on her grandmother's porch.

A few seconds of silent reminiscing passed before Hattie continued the story. "Back to Grandma's garden. That was her pride and joy, I tell ya. Yessiree. Was there anything much left of it when you bought the place?"

"Not really, I'm afraid." Darci tried to recall what had been in the yard last December. "Well, all the trees, of course. Oh, and the lilacs, one bush on each side of the house."

"I'm so glad they're still here!" Hattie appeared startled for a second, as if she'd swallowed her own tongue. "I mean, this is your place now, and of course you have a right to change anything you want. I didn't mean-"

"Don't be silly, I understand exactly what you meant," Darci cut her off. "And don't worry. Those pretty lilacs aren't going anywhere."

"Grandma had things growing in just about every square inch of this yard. Of course, there was grass in the middle," Hattie said, smiling, "but she had perennial borders, rose beds, every-day bloomers growing around the front porch, a vegetable garden, tulips and Easter flowers, a grape arbor, some kind of viney stuff covering an arch out back, and plenty of 'pee OH knees', as folks around here called peonies. She kept two ferns hanging on the front porch, just like you do."

"What a nice coincidence," Darci said, thinking Hattie and Gene didn't know the half of it.

Darci had absolutely no intention of telling them Hattie's dead grandmother haunted the flower store. No way. The thought of a loved one roaming the earth as one of the undead would be way too upsetting for anyone, and at Hattie's age, Darci feared the revelation could bring on a fainting spell or heart attack. Or they might think she was a lunatic and go running out of the building, never to tell her any more Miss Addie stories. No, Darci sealed her lips on the matter.

Hattie doted on Adelaide's accomplishments with the botanical society. "Grandma was fascinated with orchids. They were so hard to grow back then, even for a green thumb like her. That area over yonder," Hattie pointed to the porthole, "is where she used to keep her special house-plants, the ones we kids weren't allowed to mess with. She had a marble top table right in front of the window."

Darci hoped Hattie and Gene didn't see the goose bumps spring up on her arms. So that's why plants thrived in that spot. It was Miss Addie's nursery.

"We have a lot of luck with things over there, too." Darci hoped the odd smile twitching at her lips didn't make her look crazy. Since her company didn't run screaming from the room, she guessed she was safe for the time being. "Must be the light."

For the second time since their arrival, a cold spot settled over the room. Darci didn't want to draw attention to it and hoped they wouldn't notice, just in case they were up on their paranormal studies. "Sorry about the temperature. I keep meaning to have that dang air conditioner fixed."

Daisy started chirping in that special way she did when someone paid attention to her. Her tweeting had a different tone when she wanted out of the cage. Before she turned around, Darci knew the parakeet would be positioned on the front, her little pink feet wrapped around the bars as she bobbled her head, looking at someone visible only to Daisy.

"Oh, what a precious little bird," Hattie cooed as she bounced over to the cage. "Just a tweetin' away in there aren't ya, little fella."

"Little gal, actually." The cold spot grew even colder around Darci. Without a doubt in her mind, she knew Miss Addie stood beside her granddaughter. "We call her Daisy."

"Well, you just keep singing, little miss." Hattie turned her head toward Darci. "Daisies were one of Grandma's favorites. She planted enough so she could keep bouquets when they were in season, which is practically all summer."

"Really?" Darci craved a cup of Kahlua-laced
228

coffee. She was beginning to wonder whether Miss Addie had forseen Hattie's visit. Could the ghost have put ideas in her head, about Daisy's name or the library research, wanting her to know about her family before they came calling?

"Yes, they lined both sides of the house." That said, Hattie walked to the porthole, perhaps wanting to look out on the yard her grandmother had spent so much of her life tending. She came to a sudden stop, her shin even with the place Wade patched. The repair was invisible, thanks to her husband's craftsmanship, but Darci knew that was the spot.

Hattie put her fingertips against the yellow plaster, caressing the wall. Darci wondered about the *déjà vu* moment, and then it dawned on her.

Oh my God, Darci thought. That's the spot where Paxton saw the Ghost Lady doing the exact same thing, running her hand over the wall as if she were looking for something. Unsure if the chills running down her spine were from the cold spot or the oddity of what was happening, she shivered, her eyes never leaving Hattie.

"This is where it used to hang, Gene." He nodded, apparently knowing what his wife was talking about, though Darci didn't have a clue. The way things were going lately, she wouldn't be surprised to learn the Browns used to hang vampire bats there for the werewolves to play with.

Hattie faced Darci and Gene. "Grandma displayed her most prized possession right here." She pointed at the spot she'd ran her fingers over. "It was a special china plate. She hung it

229

here so everyone who entered her home could see it. Her parents brought it over on the ship when they sailed from Ireland. There was a whole set back then, a wedding gift from a favorite uncle, I believe. When Grandma got married, she asked her mother for one of the plates."

You remember! Oh, it does my old heart good to know you didn't forget about me, and you're here to help. I love you, Hattie honey. Sure do wish you could hear me.

Darci hadn't given much thought to the broken china pieces Wade fished out of the wall. He'd left them on the floor, pieced together in their original shape. Despite the pretty and unusual pattern, Darci didn't know why she couldn't bring herself to throw the shards away. Instead, she put them on a shelf in the workroom and hadn't thought about them since. Should she bring them out and give the broken dish to Hattie? Maybe it wasn't even the same plate. Darci didn't know what to do.

"I remember we stood right here looking at the serving dish and she told me all about it. Grandma said that whenever she got discouraged about anything, she'd look at the plate and run her fingers over the scalloped edge. She drew inspiration from it. She'd say 'If this fragile piece of china could cross the Atlantic Ocean in one piece, surely to goodness I can make it through whatever small crisis comes into my life'." Hattie lost herself in thought, her face the picture of serenity.

"Do you have the plate now?" Darci felt like an ass. She was afraid she knew the answer, yet had to ask.

"No, I really don't know what happened to it. I figured my aunt or uncle got it after Grandma died, so one of my cousins might've inherited it. I never gave it much thought, except to remember Grandma telling me about it. I do have a cup and saucer that match it, though."

Pride filled Hattie's voice. "The original set from Ireland got divided up between Grandma and her sisters when her parents passed away. Grandma's grandparents sent her and Grandpa a tea set that matched when they got married. Oh, they're beautiful, in the Belleek Nautilus pattern. The teacups are shaped like a big shell, the handle looks like pink coral, and two tiny little china conch shells work as feet on the front of the cup. The delicate little saucer has scalloped edges, like a clamshell. Anyway, Grandma passed them on to my aunt, and later Aunt Virginia gave me one of the cup and saucers. I keep it in a special place in the front of my curio cabinet. Bust out in a sweat whenever I spring clean, scared to death of breaking it."

Gene nodded, one side of his mouth lifted in a lopsided grin. "She's not kiddin'. She puts two layers of towels on the table to set them on while she shines 'em up. Fussed at me last time because I tried to sit down and eat a bran muffin.

'What in the world's wrong with you, Gene? Are you trying to mess up my breakables? If you knock this china off, you'll be wearing my shoe in your backside.' I had to eat my snack in the living room watchin' *The View*, and she don't usually let me eat in rooms with carpet."

"That precious Irish plate is the only thing Grandma ever threatened to tan our hides over. We took her word for it, too. If I'd broken it, I don't think I'd be able to sit down today. We never tossed a ball in here, and tiptoed around this wall. It would've broke Grandma's heart if anything happened to it."

The pained tone in Hattie's voice during that last sentence helped Darci make a decision. She thought it best not to bring up the broken pieces Wade found, afraid it would some way spoil things for Hattie. Sunlight shined through the window just then, and glinted off something on Hattie's dress Darci hadn't noticed before.

"That," Darci said, eyes widening as she pointed, about to ask another question she full well knew the answer to. "It's so pretty. Where'd you get it?"

"Grandma left it to me." Hattie's finger lovingly brushed the broach she wore near her heart. "Almost forgot I put it on today, since we were coming here. She wasn't really a jewelry person, but she wore this all the time. It was a gift after she helped deliver twins, from a Cherokee lady named Betsy. The babies barely made it, and wouldn't have without Grandma seeing to them. Back then, a lot of folks looked down on Indians,

232

but not Grandma. She and Betsy got to be real good friends, and I think they exchanged letters up to the end."

Darci stepped closer for a better look at the pin Miss Addie still wore when she showed herself. She'd never been able to make out the design details before. "It's beautiful." Tiny sage leaves made of antique silver formed a slender figure eight about two inches long.

From all the reading she'd done on herbs, the fact that sage symbolized wisdom and immortality leaped to her mind. She just might pencil in 'is a favorite of ghosts' in the margins when she got home. Another thought occurred to her. Miss Addie must have been the one who kept moving that Pow Wow flier around last month, to give her a little extra push to go, maybe so Darci could hobnob with the descendants of the Cherokee friend who gave her the pin.

"I guess we'd better be on our way, and get out of yours," Hattie said after glancing at her watch.

No, you cain't leave yet! Time is precious and there's no tellin' when I'll get a chance to be with you again. Why cain't I make you see me? I'm tryin' so hard, and you're my own flesh and blood.

My tears won't stop, I cain't help it. Only thing I can do is hug you, and pray the good lord lets you feel it. I love you, Hattie.

Darci walked Hattie and Gene out, after they

finally managed to pry open the front door. She made a mental note to have Hoyt squirt the lock and hinges with WD-40.

"Thanks so much for lettin' us visit. It sure did mean a lot to me." Suddenly overcome by emotion, tears flowed down Hattie's cheeks and past her sweet smile. Gene's handkerchief came in handy again. "It feels almost like Grandma's still here. Might sound silly, but I thought I smelled her perfume a few seconds ago, rose and amber with a hint of vanilla. Haven't sniffed that in years."

Darci felt compelled to give her a hug, which she did, then waved as they walked down the sidewalk. "Y'all stop by and have lunch with me the next time you're in the area." They promised and she hoped to see them again soon.

She watched their car pull out of the driveway and ease down Main Street. "You have a lovely granddaughter, Miss Addie. It's easy to see how proud she is of you." The shop had stayed cold the whole time Hattie talked about the plate and reminisced. The familiar presence in the room didn't spook Darci in the slightest.

Daisy chirped and bobbed herself into a frenzy. Since the ghost wasn't likely to open the cage, Darci answered the parakeet's request. Daisy hopped onto her finger and sidestepped up to her shoulder. She stretched her little yellow-feathered head out toward empty air, as if reaching for an unseen hand.

Roy Nolan's trial didn't last long, given his confession and the overwhelming evidence against him.

Darci sat in the courtroom, relieved to have her testimony over and done with. Her time on the stand the day before had been nerve wracking, to say the least. She'd absentmindedly fidgeted with her bracelet as she answered questions, first as an expert witness regarding the *Ricinus communis* in Teresa Nolan's yard. That was the easy part. The second half of her testimony, when she established herself as the victim of attempted murder, was even worse for her. She was conscious of each word that came out of her mouth, especially the ones she omitted about the bells on the door drawing her attention to make her stand up right before the first shot. No way in hell did she plan to swear under oath that Miss Addie's ghost existed, even if she had saved her life. Though she didn't think belief in the paranormal would necessarily land her in the nuthouse, she was afraid it might make her a little less creditable. And she would never hear the end of it.

Beside her now, Wade clenched his jaw each time he looked toward the back of Roy Nolan's head.

The coroner, an arresting officer from Ohio, and a psychologist the defense team obviously hoped would declare Roy insane-which he had not-also testified previously. So had Belinda Blanford, who melted into a hot squalling mess, swearing she didn't know a damn thing about poisoned food or Roy killing anybody. Hysterical, she begged the judge not to lock her up, even though no charge for accessory to murder had ever been filed against her.

Eddie Miller had just left the stand after pointing to the man he saw drive away in a blue pickup after the shooting.

The prosecutor submitted Ashley Rosales' sworn statement into evidence, her name withheld from the general court due to her being a minor, and to keep her identity from the goons who roughed Roy up in the stables that day in March. Darci could only imagine how horrified the poor girl must've been, hiding in the stall overhearing that conversation. Cyril Maldonado had personally helped Ashley with her horse therapy while she recovered from the hit-and-run accident, and to learn the man she respected and revered died at Roy's hands because of a stupid gambling debt must have been devastating. She'd kept the incident a secret for fear that those same thugs-the ones who cut the brakes on Roy's mother's car and stood punching Nolan on the other side of the barn-would kill her to keep her mouth shut, if they ever found out what she knew. Thank God they hadn't seen her.

Roy mostly just stared at the floor during the entire hearing.

"The prosecution calls Sheriff Maxwell Roberts as its next witness." Dressed in a gray suit and baby blue tie, Henry Dawson looked over his papers as the bailiff swore Max in. After a while, he questioned Max on the subject of evidence.

"My deputies and I spent a few hours search-
ing Nolan's house on August twenty-first, the day
he was seen leaving the scene after he shot at
Darci Shelton." Max paused to glare at Roy, who
continued to stare at the floor. "We got a warrant
right after Darci explained why she had reason to
believe Roy was the shooter. One of the pans we
bagged for evidence came back from the lab positive for traces of poison. Since ricin isn't the type
of ingredient anyone in their right mind would
cook with, that pretty much proved Roy'd poison
Cyril. Yep, Nolan sure thinks he's a big man,
what with making sure his best friend died a
slow, painful death, then him trying to kill a hard
working woman because she figured out what he
did. That son of a bitch-"

"Objection!" The defense attorney jumped to
his feet as Henry Dawson shushed Max.

"Sustained." The judge banged his gavel until
the courtroom fell silent. "Sheriff, you know better than to carry on like this on the witness
stand. Any more foul language and I'll find you in
contempt."

Dawson whispered something to Max, who
struggled to get his temper under control before
he continued his testimony.

"We searched M & N Stables next, but didn't
turn anything up. The Styrofoam plate from the
diner most likely ended up in the dumpster the
day Roy poisoned Cyril. By now, it'd be at the
bottom of the Webster County landfill under a
ton of used toilet paper and refuse."

Cyril's wife was the last witness later that day.

Mrs. Maldonado slapped Roy in the face on her way to the witness stand. Nobody blamed her for hitting him. By the time the lone bailiff in the courtroom got to her, Nolan's sobbed apology drew his attention away from the widow.

"I'm so sorry Pauline, I didn't want to do it." Tears dripped off Roy's face, his ragged sobs making it hard for him to speak. He ignored his lawyer's plea for him to hush. "I loved Cyril like a brother, you know that. They were gonna kill Mama, and the life insurance was the only way I could get that much money. I thought he'd die real quick, not linger in agony like he did. It killed me to watch him suffer in his hospital bed."

His lawyer tried unsuccessfully to put Roy back in his seat. The bailiff held Mrs. Maldonado up, a comforting arm around her shoulder as she listened to Roy's confession.

"When Mama told me about Mrs. Shelton stopping by asking about that castor plant, I knew she'd figured out what I'd done. That damn fruity-ass Donovan Lewis told her all about Belinda bringing me the takeout boxes, and I knew she'd spill everything to the sheriff. He's her uncle or some relation, I think. I would've done anything to keep from going to jail."

By this point, the entire courtroom was silent. The defense lawyer gave up, threw his pen down on the table, and crossed his arms. The judge motioned to two officers in the back.

"Mama's gonna be fine now, 'cause I paid off what I owed." The officers dragged Roy from the room.

Court adjourned for the day.

Celia Kemp covered the trial for the local newspaper. For the first degree murder of Cyril Maldonado and the attempted murder of Darci Shelton, Roy Nolan was sentenced to life in prison with no possibility of parole.

"I'll get the nominations." Charlotte retrieved the wooden box decoupaged with Victorian cutouts of botanicals, birds, and insects from its spot on the table beside the front door. She brought it back to the kitchen, where she and Darci took a midmorning coffee break.

Once a month, they drew a name from the box to reward some deserving citizen with a basket or fresh arrangement. People could submit nominations through Petal Pushers' website or in the shop.

They did draw the winner out, along with losing entries, but that wasn't exactly how their selection process worked. Darci set up the award to recognize people who did exceptional deeds for others, and those who needed cheering up during hard times. The decision to read through all the nominees and choose the most deserving came in January when, on their first draw, they pulled a slip of paper that said something to the effect of 'Pick Janie, cuz she's my friend and super cool'.

On this November morning, Charlotte divided the nominations and dug in to her half. "Can't wait to see what we find this time."

Zingers sometime found their way into the box, like 'Lady GaGa rules' or 'Spiderman for Mayor'. Charlotte's all-time personal favorite read, 'We vote for the blonde chick with big hooters behind the counter', which most likely came from one of the teenage boys who stopped by to see Hoyt.

"Here we go." Darci separated the slips of paper into groups as she read through her half. "This pile is for entries saying so and so is very nice or special or sweet and deserves to win, minus any real reason. Cranks go on the corner, after being read out loud and laughed at."

"Okay, and people who do something extraordinary go beside the salt shaker," Charlotte added, plunking down an entry. "And the pepper people are depressed or going through a rough patch."

After they finished sorting each month, they put the best candidates from the salt and pepper piles in the center of the table. They debated over these until they reached a decision. Past winners included a couple who lost their home in a tornado and a local man who ran an animal rescue for abandoned dog, cats, and other pets who needed a home.

"Let's have one more Krispy Kreme, to help us make our final choice." Darci handed Charlotte a donut, fall themed with chocolate icing and orange sprinkles, before taking a bite herself. "Mmmm," she said through a mouthful, "glad this was my day to splurge."

"I think the winner's obvious this time. Laura DeMoss gets my vote." Charlotte raked up the crumbs accumulating in front of her and piled them on top of the crank stack, destined for the garbage can. "With all her volunteer work, she should get the Nobel Peace Prize."

"She's my pick, too. Donates time at the homeless shelter and lets destitute women use her home address and phone number on job applications, since they need a permanent address to get hired. The stuff about her literacy program sealed the deal." Darci tapped the newspaper article paperclipped to the nomination form.

"It's too bad she doesn't get one red dime for all the time she spends helping other people," Charlotte added. "Laura DeMoss just does it out of the goodness of her heart."

"We'll fill her prize basket with stuff she can use to pamper herself for a change. I'm thinking lotions, cushy slippers, and," the wheels in Darci's head spun out of control, "we need to make a mall run."

Later that afternoon, Hoyt left to deliver Ms. DeMoss's prize, one of the best Darci and Charlotte ever put together. A fluffy lavender robe and matching slippers filled a huge wicker basket, with lotions, oils, bubble bath, and two lilac-scented candles nestled inside. Charlotte tied a wispy raffia bow to the handle and Darci tucked two small ceramic guardian angels between the folds of velvety fabric. Well worth the effort for someone who so clearly deserved it.

Darci balanced the books at the end of November, reminded once again of her fast-approaching deadline. Would this New Year's Eve be the worst day of her life or mark a milestone in her career?

The black ink penned in the ledger gave her cause to hope. If December went as well as the previous two months, with no unexpected losses, Petal Pushers would show a profit. She fidgeted with a rubber band, afraid to get her hopes up, terrified to think about the consequences if she didn't make it. This shop was a dream come true, not just a way to earn a living. She needed to prove herself capable of financial independence, since her biggest fear was for history to repeat itself. How had her mother found the strength to fight a losing battle against poverty when her husband died, leaving her with a daughter to feed and a mountain of debt?

Darci crossed the fingers she'd nearly worked to the bone, and prayed for a reason to celebrate.

**Petal Pushers' Plant of the Month for
November is**

Impatiens
Impatiens wallerana
Annual

Common name: Everyday Bloomers, Busy Lizzie, and Jewelweeds

Brief description: Impatiens are my all time favorite bedding plant, and I do believe Bernice from Golden Days Retirement Home mentioned they're her favorite, as well. They grow from eight to twenty inches tall and have cute little flowers that bloom nonstop from early summer until the fall frost. The flowers come in a variety of colors and combinations.

Symbolism: motherly love

Trivia: Most people buy these as bedding plants, but an interesting and little known fact is that impatiens can, at times, produce pods that scatter seeds up to twenty feet when they pop.

Growing instructions: Everyday Bloomers thrive in full shade, but can do pretty well in more sun. These wilt if they dry out, so keep them watered in the summer heat.

Uses: Impatiens make wonderful additions to flower beds, in containers and hanging baskets, planted under trees, and as houseplants. They add a nice splash of color wherever you need it.

Tools & Tips: Don't forget to plant bulbs now for pretty flowers in the late winter and spring. Plant bulbs for tulips, daffodils, crocuses, etc. about six weeks before the ground freezes. How the heck will you know when that is, you ask. It's usually right after the first heavy frost, or when the night temperature stays between 40 and 50 degrees.

Chapter Twelve

December

Earth laughs in flowers.
~ Ralph Waldo Emerson

"Business is a boomin'," Darci told Charlotte over the din of shoppers. The holiday season kept a constant stream of customers flowing through Petal Pushers in search of Christmas décor and gifts.

Wade and Paxton did their part to help out, with truckloads of pinecones and fresh boughs from their biweekly trips to the woods. Sometimes they found mistletoe, the only problem being that it grew so high up in the trees. Darci wondered if she could sell the sprigs of mistletoe for a dollar more if she advertised that real live woodsmen shot it down from a tree.

She and Charlotte turned the pine branches into swags, mantle sprays, and wreaths. Decorated to fit every style imaginable, each wreath type had its own unique name, to avoid confusion with online orders. 'The Minimalist' was a circle of greenery with a big red bow on the bottom, while 'The Standard' referred to wreaths with glass balls and a smaller red or green bow. Charlotte made dozens of her favorite 'Jingle Bell' wreaths with assorted sleigh bells strung on sturdy lengths of wire, looped into a circle that donned a red ribbon and raffia bow. They whipped up 'After School Specials' with tiny Santas, snowflakes, and a few crayons for added color.

"Internet sales are through the roof." The printer spit out the latest orders while Darci updated Petal Pushers' website with new pictures of their Christmas creations. The five pages devoted to wreaths racked up the most hits. Online orders had Hoyt running to the post office a couple times a day, sending packages all over the country. "I knew it was a good idea to specialize in something particular and go heavy on the advertising."

"You're a regular marketing whiz." Charlotte patted her cousin on the back. "Between the newspaper ads, eBay, and those fliers you paid Hoyt's girlfriend to put on windshields, we're busier than a pack of prune fed cats covering up kitty turds."

"This *is* a team effort, don't forget. You and Hoyt came up with ideas for those novelty wreaths that fly off the shelves."

'The Gothic' featured black bows and tiny silver snowflakes, their delicate presence adding a classic feel anyone who wore black lipstick could appreciate. Japanese figurines peeped out of the 'Manga', inspired by the Asian craze in comics and cartoons. For the 'Sports Nut', little baseballs, basketballs, footballs, and soccer balls mingled with coach whistles spray-painted gold. Hair salons snatched up 'A Curly Christmas', made with multicolored perm rollers from the beauty supply store. 'John Deere' wreaths decorated with a green and gold bow, red glass orbs, and miniature tractors were one of the hottest items. Their 'Pet Wreath' assortment featured dog biscuits and squeaky toys, catnip filled mice and feathers, or bird treats and millet, designed to be taken apart and fed to lucky pets after the holidays. Darci's stomach growled each time she put together 'Sweet Tooth' wreaths, jam-packed with mini Hershey bars, gold and silver foiled Kisses, and candy canes, topped off with a bow made from red licorice vines.

"I still can't believe the 'Nympho Deluxe' you came up with." Darci'd laughed at that sight until tears spilled over her lashes, but she flat out refused to let Charlotte sell it. "Something is definitely wrong with you."

"Oh, come on, Darce. Prophylactics and pasties might draw in a more diverse crowd." Charlotte flashed her mischievous grin. "Okay, so I'm a closet pervert, what can I say. Jimbo liked it though. I hung that one up in our bedroom and not ten minutes later he-"

"Oh, no no no," Darci interrupted, shaking her finger in her cousin's face. "You promised I didn't have to hear any details about that. Y'all keep going at this rate and little Cole will have a house full of brothers and sisters, not to mention his sex-crazed parents."

When Darci opened the shop one morning, she found something strange. Far beyond the Mac Daddy of all weird coincidences, this could only be solid proof of Miss Addie's ghostly presence.

The same book had, once again, fallen off the shelf and landed front cover up on the floor. An empty space between the other volumes marked the absence of *Garden Art Mosaics*. She squatted to retrieve it, but drew her hand back to cover her mouth instead.

Positioned on the center of the book, a shard of china dared her to deny its existence. Darci couldn't bring herself to touch it.

She darted to the workroom and the broken plate. Everything was as she'd left it, the pieces still positioned like a worked puzzle. The shard that should occupy the center was missing even though all the others remained exactly as they had been.

With shaky hands, she pulled her camera from a drawer. She routinely photographed her arrangements and centerpieces to put in an album customers could flip through to see examples of her work. Now she took a picture of the plate pieces, then a shot of the shard lying on the garden art book, still untouched on the floor.

She knew Charlotte would believe her, and Hoyt, since he'd been pale faced and pretty shaken last week when he saw "some damn disappearing old chick", then swore he wasn't on anything. The pictures were more for her own peace of mind, for later, when she might look back on this morning and doubt her sanity. She also hoped they might help convince Wade she hadn't hallucinated.

She put away the camera and turned the sign in the front window around so that 'Open' greeted the front porch. Back behind the counter, she stared at the book on the floor for a while, then, holding her breath, moved it onto the counter. She poked the antique pottery shard with the tip of her index finger, halfway expecting it to spin through the air like something from *The Exorcist*.

Darci screamed, jerking her hand away as she jumped backward. She tripped over the office chair and landed on her ass.

"Damn phone! Nearly scared me to death." The caller ordered flowers for a relative recuperating from gall bladder surgery while Darci rubbed the seat of her pants, sure she'd have one hell of a bruise on her butt cheek. She hung up the receiver and shifted her thoughts back to the matter at hand.

A fragment of Miss Addie's favorite possession, an heirloom brought to this country from Ireland when her family immigrated, sat atop *Garden Art Mosaics*, the same book that kept mysteriously jumping off the shelf. It didn't take a rocket scientist to figure out what the ghost was trying to tell her.

"Well, Miss Addie," Darci said to the room, empty but for herself and an invisible apparition. "I take it you'd like me to use your broken Belleek to make something pretty."

She looked around the room, wondering if she'd get an answer. Nothing happened, except Daisy started to chirp. A knowing smile tugged the edges of Darci's mouth.

"Sounds like a great idea to me." She tilted her head in thought. "We'll make something indestructible, so you won't have to worry about your mama's china."

Darci put the shard back with its counterparts in the workroom, afraid someone might accidentally throw it away if left on the counter out front. Seated at the desk under the back window, she flipped through the book full of instructions on creating mosaic pieces for the home and garden. Page after page held so many beautiful photographs, she didn't know how she'd ever make up her mind.

A bead of water plopped onto the open book. "What the hell?" The glistening droplet seemed to stare back at her from the glossy page.

A glance at the dry ceiling above ruled out a drip, plus it hadn't rained for the past week. A cold chill settled around her and drove another possibility through her brain.

"Um, Miss Addie? Is this another sign from you?"

Her eyes scanned the shop for anything out of the ordinary, perhaps a ghostly figure in a Victorian dress. She laughed at how stupid the idea seemed.

Bells jingled, drawing her attention up front where she expected to see a customer stroll in. Her gaze met a closed door instead, the bells attached to it still jingling away.

"Okay, I get it." The ringing stopped. Darci swiveled her chair back around to her desk and studied the damp page. "Great idea, Miss Addie."

Hoyt picked up the supplies she asked for at a craft store on his way to work that afternoon. After reimbursing him for the expense, Darci got busy on the project.

The mosaic process was a lot of fun, like working a puzzle made from bits of porcelain. With the pieces arranged on the worktable, there was virtually no way to mess up the grouting. Darci fought the urge to take it home to show Wade, but the project needed to set and dry overnight.

"Oh my gosh. You made that!" Charlotte exclaimed when she came to work the next morning. "It looks like something you'd pay a fortune for at an art show. I can't believe you put that together using a bunch of broken junk. Amazing."

"It does look pretty nice there, doesn't it? Just what the wall needed." The only logical place for it was where the original plate had hung, just above eye level on the shop wall, between the porthole and the shelving. Darci stood back to admire her handiwork, pretty proud of herself. More importantly, she knew Miss Addie would approve.

Customers raved about the new clock, and a

few offered to buy it. "Oh, no," Darci answered each time. "That's our new family heirloom." Pride swelled her heart at the thought of Miss Addie passing it down to her.

The clockworks in the center nearly faded into the background of the mosaic. The pewter hands and numbers stood out against the dark cream base. Around the apple-sized faceplate lay the focal point of the clock-the pieces of Belleek china. Nipped to a uniform size, the fragments arranged on the clock base measured a bit larger in diameter than the original plate. Grout a shade darker than the pewter numbers filled in the blank spaces.

"Guess what I used for a border around the outer edge?" Darci asked Ashley when she complimented the new clock. She'd stopped by Petal Pushers on her way to babysit Cole, to post a new SADD poster in the shop window. Charlotte lucked out when she hired her.

"Marbles maybe? Or beads?"

"Nope, not even close. It's pea gravel," Darci said, watching for her reaction. Addie Brown's rose garden had been gone for decades, but the tiny stones remained, buried beneath mud and grass. "Dug it out of the ground with a trowel, soaked 'em in bleach, then scrubbed 'em clean until the original luster shined through."

"You're kidding." Ashley leaned in for a closer look at the clock. "My art teacher would so drool all over himself if he saw this. What made you think to use pea gravel?"

"It just seemed like the right thing to add a little detail. I think they look kind of like little pearls lined up around the edge."

Darci ran her fingers over the mosaic each afternoon before she locked up. To her, it symbolized Miss Addie's timelessness, her ability to link the past to the present and future. The pewter hands ticked minutes away into infinity. The antique china was a link to the past and Addie's Irish roots. The rose garden pebbles represented the earth they'd been a part of for thousands of years. Yep, she thought as she gazed at the clock, Miss Addie would love and appreciate the piece, and hopefully realize it stood as a tribute to her, as well.

A cold spot settled over the room like a chilly hug. The Ghost Lady still haunted the shop even after her plate was back in one piece, so Darci ruled out her coming around for unfinished business. She believed Adelaide Brown wanted to stay in the home she loved so much, the building she seemed to make sure fell into Darci's hands to become Petal Pushers. Miss Addie would likely remain as much a permanent fixture as the roof, the staircase, and the tribute clock.

Daisy chirped.

"You're just oozing confidence, Hon." Wade watched Darci gather sketches of floral arrangements off the foyer table and sling her purse across her shoulder.

She'd shrugged off the compliment, but pecked

a kiss from his cheek before she headed to work. Now she stood behind the counter at Petal Pushers, thinking back over all she'd accomplished during the past year. Wade's words might just hold more truth than flattery.

Darci always tried her best to do a quality job on a professional level. The first two months after the grand opening, she rushed to the store worried over whether or not she'd sell anything she'd invested so much time, energy, and cash into making.

Somewhere between Labor Day and Thanksgiving, something changed. The alarm clock no longer triggered a rush of panic. She greeted the day with a smile, eager to eat breakfast and open the shop. Enthusiasm replaced anxiety each time she flipped the sign in the shop window to 'Open'. She looked forward to her workdays like some people looked forward to a vacation or the first cocktail at the end of a busy week.

Dread of bills and mortgage payments slipped away, which let her spend more time planning advertisements and specials. She did the dishes after supper daydreaming about what might go on in the shop the following day, who may come in, or what type of arrangements she could whip up next.

The biggest change she saw in herself, however, was confidence that she wouldn't screw everything up. Darci grinned at the realization. She looked forward to placing orders for plants, fresh flowers, and supplies. Indecisive as ever about choices over which varieties in which colors and how many to purchase, the selection process now went the way she really wanted, rather than which were on sale.

Charlotte boosted Darci's confidence to another level after she watched her make a sale one afternoon. "Do you realize how much your approach to customers has changed?"

"What do you mean?" Darci leaned against the counter, waiting for a punch line.

"Well, the chit-chat and small talk always did come easy for you," Charlotte said, looking Darci in the eye. "You're just more self-assured and relaxed now. You used to be like, 'The yellow roses would be pretty, I think, unless you'd prefer the red or pink. Any of those would be good choices. What do you think? Is the yellow a good pick for you?'"

Darci smiled at the imitation, knowing the timid sales pitch was probably accurate.

"But now you're all like, 'Since you're looking for roses, I'd suggest these beautiful yellow ones. Here, give 'em a sniff. Heavenly, aren't they? How many would you like in that bouquet?'"

"You might have me confused with Martha Stewart." Darci beamed, and couldn't think of anything else to say.

Darci sat down to balance the books in the middle of December. She reached to take a pen from the holder and knocked over an old bottle of antacid tablets. She used to pop those things by the handful when she got sick at her stomach from paying bills, something she now viewed as a simple task she could do with Daisy singing on her shoulder. Calculator in hand, she started crunching numbers.

Screams brought Charlotte and Hoyt running in from the back to see what was wrong.

Darci pranced around the room, lifting her knees as she pumped her arms toward the ceiling. She kept saying things like "Woo hoo", "Oh yeah", and "Hot diggity damn".

"Are you having some kind of fit," Charlotte asked, shooting her a skeptical grin, "or did Happy Hour come early today?"

Darci felt as giddy as a five-year-old set loose in a candy shop. She danced around them, pausing twice to 'raise the roof'.

"We did it! We showed a profit, oh yes we did. I met my goal in spite of all the setbacks." Darci performed her own unique version of the Cabbage Patch. "Petal Pushers officially gets to stay open. Woo hoo!"

Hoyt turned on the radio, then he and Charlotte joined in the celebration.

"Did you ever really doubt you'd make it?" Charlotte asked Darci as Hoyt dipped her backwards. "You always do whatever you set your mind to."

"Not really. Remember the whole diet thing, my plan to lose twenty pounds before last summer? Didn't happen. Please note," Darci said, sweeping her hands down her torso like a game show model showcasing a shiny new dishwasher. Then she

turned around and shook her rear end in Charlotte's direction.

"Oh, you know you look just fine the way you
are," Charlotte chided. "And with this shop being
so important, I never doubted you for a second."

"Congratulations, Boss Lady. I always kinda
knew you'd come through, too."

Flo Rida probably never envisioned the bizarre
do-si-do they danced to his music.

"Oh, I had plenty of doubts," Darci confessed.
"Doubts with cold chills each time we lost money,
waking up from nightmares of Scrooge coming to
throw me and poor little Daisy out in the snow as
he foreclosed on the shop. Yep, plenty of doubts,
but now that's over, thank God."

Darci pulled a couple bills from the cash register. "We need to celebrate. Hoyt, my dear boy,
would you be so kind as to run down to Krispy
Kreme and pick up two dozen donuts? Assorted
ones, and don't you dare skimp on the chocolate
and goo."

Hoyt took the money and headed for the door,
pausing to take his jacket from the coat rack.

"I'll put on a fresh pot of coffee," Charlotte offered.

"Good idea. We'll eat our fill, then put the rest
out for the customers. It's a shame I didn't have a
chance to advertise the freebies."

During their celebratory donut fest, they discussed the year's highs and lows, and some of
their favorite customers. An idea popped into
Darci's head.

"I think I'm going to throw a party. A one-year

customer appreciation bash. We'll have it here on New Year's Eve, in the afternoon, of course, so it doesn't interfere with all the other shindigs going on that night."

"Cool. But I think the theme should be focused more toward you and your awesome success." Hoyt bit into a chocolate-iced custard donut, then wiped his mouth with a napkin. "Oh man, now I see why you're so into the whole Krispy Kreme thing. These things are off the hook."

"It's kind of like how rock stars thank their fans when they accept awards. Without the fans, who'd listen to their music? For us, we owe the gratitude to the customers. Think about it. They're the ones who keep Petal Pushers in business."

"Good point, Darce." Charlotte reached out to smack Hoyt's hand away from the last custard donut. "Hey, I called dibs on that. Here, you try this one. It's shaped like Frosty the Snowman."

"Vicious." Hoyt rubbed his hand, grinned, and then bit the head off the snowman donut. "Sure do wish Frosty had custard guts."

After she filled the latest orders for holiday wreathes, Darci sat down at the computer to design an invitation style flier. The more she thought about the party, the more excited she got.

She wiped her eyes with a tissue. This was a time for celebration, not crying, even though these were tears of joy. She couldn't believe she'd actually done it. Scrimping and saving, she took the money she earned working a retail job she hated and invested every dime, along with the money from her business loan, into Petal Pushers. The total she read on the ledger today still seemed like a dream, a very happy one she didn't want to wake up from. Not only were they in the black, she showed a profit! The loan would still take a few more years to pay off, but that was fine. Even with the setbacks, like the van repairs and those damn Dutch bulbs, Petal Pushers consistently brought in more money than expenses.

Never again would she worry about going through the same struggles her mother went through, working overtime at two jobs just to keep a roof over their heads and food on the table after Darci's father died. She reached for another Kleenex. This time she let the tears of relief wash down her face before she mopped them away.

Thanks to an active lifestyle and good genes, Wade's health was pretty much perfect, which gave Darci no logical reason to worry about him. Unless some psychopath decided to use him for target practice, that is. Her fingers found the small scar on her forehead, then she put the whole shooting incident out of her mind.

Now she'd proven she could, in fact, support her son, should tragedy ever strike her family. She could stop waking up in a cold sweat from nightmares of herself and Paxton in line at the soup kitchen, barefoot and coatless in the falling snow.

She arrived at Petal Pushers bright and early on New Year's Eve to decorate and make last minute preparations. During lunch with Charlotte, Darci floated on cloud nine.

"Today I feel like I've come full circle. We opened on New Year's Day and here it is, the last day of the year, and we're celebrating our success."

"I think it's cute how you keep saying 'we' instead of 'I'," Charlotte said. "Hoyt and me are just your little peons, you know. All the success is due to you, the sole proprietor of this joint."

"Well, I couldn't have stayed in business by myself." Darci shook her head. "You worked as hard as I did, and had a baby to boot. Hoyt made deliveries and stuff, Wade did all the repairs, and little Paxton helped with the watering, even if he was kind of overenthusiastic about it."

"And Daisy added ambiance with her chirping, if you want to dig that far." Charlotte rolled her eyes.

"Yeah, and don't forget Miss Addie," Darci added, not catching Charlotte's sarcasm. "She did her part by saving the sick plants. You-"

The jingling bells ended their lunch and signaled the arrival of a steady stream of guests.

By one-thirty, Petal Pushers was packed with people. Donovan and his life partner Bradley talked about fly fishing with Wade and Jimbo. Pauline Maldonado cooed to Cole while he sucked down a bottle in Charlotte's arms. Ashley Rosales and her mother stood in front of one end of the display table, loaded down today with finger sandwiches and an array of refreshments instead of flower arrangements. Mabel and Bernice struck up a conversation with Darci's mom and Grandma Odette while Vera Tompkins chatted with Mae Roberts about an event scheduled at the retirement home. Hattie and Gene stood by the porthole telling Laura DeMoss all about her grandmother's African violets and orchids. Paxton played catch with his friend Jake out in the backyard, though their winter coats and scarves made them a little less dexterous than usual.

Max joined the party late, and gave Darci a peck on the cheek after he waved to his wife across the room. "Congrats on your first year in the floral business, even though I still wish you'd let me deputize you."

"Thanks Max, but I don't think you'd want my clumsy fingers wrapped around a thirty-eight special," Darci said, smiling up at him.

"I'd be willing to take my chances. Anybody with the talent to make real flowers bloom outside, in Kentucky, in January, has my vote of confidence."

As Max strolled away, Darci couldn't figure out what the hell he was talking about. She'd brought in the ferns from the porch two months ago. Not much of anything could grow outside here this time of year.

Curious, she made her way to the porthole to look for whatever Max thought he'd seen. Maybe he had some New Year's hootch before he came over, though she doubted he'd get tipsy during the day, especially not on duty.

"Oh my God." Darci couldn't believe her eyes.

Snow was starting to fall, bits of white fluff sticking to the crunchy brown grass on the lawn. Along the side of the shop, exactly where Hattie had mentioned two months before, stood a row of daisies, fresh blooms atop crisp green stems. Snowflakes settled on their leaves, but they didn't show any signs of wilting under the cold. This was simply not possible, though she was looking right at it. The sound of Daisy chirping echoed in her ears, and her shoulders chilled, as if some unseen arm was hugging her.

She desperately hoped Charlotte brought some booze.

"They're beautiful, Miss Addie. Thank you so much."

Bless your heart, Darci, I'm tickled you like 'em. Just like my Hattie said, daisies have always been my favorite. It took some doin' and purt near wore me out, but this is my way of sayin' thank you for everything you've done. My home is beautiful again and brimmin' with flowers, thanks to you, but most of all, I hope you know how much that clock you made out of Mama's plate means to me. I know you cain't hear me, but I think you feel my gratitude.

Folks would be plum stupid not to do business with you, 'specially after they see our daisies a sproutin' up through the snow. I've been remembering a few things here lately, bad things that need to be set right. There's plenty for me to attend to, but I'll make it a point not to get too busy to help you keep things up around here. I cain't wait to see what we accomplish this year.

A crowd of people milled through the shop. Darci didn't know all their names, but she had a ball listening to them talk about all the ways Petal Pushers had touched their lives. Now she stood behind the counter and took a second to look around her, overwhelmed by the room full of love and friendship.

Her eyes turned to the clock she made from Miss Addie's plate. She couldn't fight the urge to let her fingers trace the mosaic. Darci hoped Petal Pushers would be as timeless, her legacy to pass down to Paxton one day, and him to his children, the way most families pass an heirloom down from one generation to the next.

"Happy New Year, everybody!" Darci beamed at the room full of people she'd come to call friends over the past twelve months. She felt good things on the horizon and looked forward to another great year. "Thanks for making Petal Pushers a success."

Under her breath, in a barely audible whisper, she said, "Happy New Year, Miss Addie." Cool air settled around her like a chilly embrace.

Daisy chirped and bobbled her head.

Petal Pushers' Plant of the Month for December is

African Violet
Saintpaulia hybrids
Perennial houseplant

Brief description: African violets are at the top of the list for popular houseplants. They're relatively easy to care for, have beautiful flowers and fuzzy green foliage, and they bloom year round, even now, with the December snow falling outside. They come in so many colors, sizes, and bloom styles, it's no wonder people love to collect them.

Symbolism: modesty, virtue, and affection.

Trivia: The African violet can give you more bang for your buck, if you like free plants. It's so easy to propagate them from leaf cuttings, just snip off a healthy leaf and stick it in water or damp soil until roots form. Then pot it and *voila*, a new free plant. Simple as that.

Growing instructions: These plants need bright sunlight, but not intense direct sun, so an east-facing window would be perfect. Keep the soil moist, but avoid getting the leaves wet or they'll turn brown. Remove wilted blooms and brown leaves to encourage new growth.

Uses: Pot African violets in pretty containers, or even in china teacups, and set them on your windowsill. Which reminds me, I'm looking for some teacups in the Belleek Nautilus pattern. If you run across any at a flea market, bring 'em in and I'll trade you for one plant or arrangement of your choice.

Tools & Tips: If your green thumbs are fretting because they're stuck in wool mittens instead of garden soil, I know just the thing for you. Now's the time to cuddle up with your colorful plant catalogs and magazines and start planning next year's garden projects. Cut out pictures of new flowers you want to grow, order up some seeds, and sketch out ideas for that bare spot in the backyard.

Don't worry! Spring will be here before you know it.

Plant and Recipe Index

Acknowledgements

For all the folks from TheNextBigWriter.com. This book never would've been published without your help, critique, advice, and support. A special shout out to Nathan B. Childs, Jessica Chambers, Natalee Binda, Linda Lee, Cathy Jones, Nancy Smith, John Van Cott, Charles Brass, and jmd.

The staff and community at NaNoWriMo, who are responsible for getting thousands of people, myself included, to write the first draft of a whole novel in thirty short days each November. And aside from the sleep deprivation, it's actually fun!

The Louisville Romance Writers for welcoming me into the chapter, an awesome group of inspiring ladies I've already learned so much from.

Most importantly, I want to thank my family for their love and support: my kids, Amanda, Brittany, and Tyler, the first to know about my writing projects, your encouragement means everything to me; my husband, Barry; my parents, Tommy and Jan Cole; my grandparents, Bobby W. and Edna E. Brown, and the late Thomas and Nancy Cole; and my brother, Jason, nephew, Trevor and niece, Chanler. Y'all made me the person I am today, heaven help you, and are partially responsible for my twisted sense of humor.

Note: I wanted to point out that the story is set in a totally fictionalized version of my hometown. The real Dixon, Kentucky, is a wonderful place to live, populated by the friendliest people you'd ever want to meet, but without the murder, and sadly, no Krispy Kreme as of yet.

About the Author

Photo courtesy of Brittany Hayes

Tina D.C. Hayes writes romantic suspense and cozy mysteries. She lives in western Kentucky with her husband and three children. A few very pampered pooches and two parrots keep her busy, but guard against writer's block.

http://tinadchayes.wordpress.com
http://twitter.com/Tina_DC_Hayes